W9-ABT-812

The Adventures of Charlie Pierce

>—◆—⊙—◆—<

The Last Egret

by Harvey E. Oyer III

Illustrations by James Balkovek

Map Illustration by Jeanne Brady

www.TheAdventuresofCharliePierce.com

Become a friend of Charlie Pierce on **Facebook**

MIDDLE
RIVER
PRESS

All rights reserved. No part of this book may be reproduced or transmitted in any form or by any means, electronic or mechanical, including photocopying, recording, or by any information storage and retrieval system, without written permission from the author, except for the inclusion of brief quotations in a review.

ISBN 978-0-9817036-8-8
0-9817036-8-2

Copyright © 2010 by Harvey E. Oyer III

Published by:
Middle River Press
1498 NE 30th Ct.
Oakland Park FL 33334
middleriverpress.com.
info@middleriverpress.com
Printed in the U.S.A.
Second printing

Dedication

To Monique

Acknowledgments

I wish to acknowledge the dedicated, outstanding work of editor Jon VanZile, illustrator James Balkovek, map illustrator Jeanne Brady, and the folks at Middle River Press. I also want to acknowledge the writings of Charles W. Pierce, from which I take many of the stories contained herein. My special thanks to Sally Conyne and S. Joyce King for their review of the manuscript and helpful suggestions.

Marco Ruiz

Introduction

This book is the second in a series of books about the adventures of young Charlie Pierce, one of South Florida's earliest pioneer settlers. The story follows Charlie's adventures as a child and teenager in the late 1800s, when South Florida was America's last frontier. Together with his Seminole friend, Tiger, Charlie experienced one of the most intriguing and exotic lives imaginable. His adventures as a young boy growing up in the wild, untamed jungles of Florida became legendary. Perhaps no other person experienced firsthand as many important events and met as many influential characters in South Florida's history.

For more information about Charlie Pierce and his adventures, go to **www.TheAdventuresofCharliePierce.com** Become a friend of Charlie Pierce on **Facebook**

Table of Contents

Chapter One

Two Pounds of Grits

I was walking on the wild end of Hypoluxo Island, where we lived, when I thought I saw the ghost.

Papa had sent me for a load of firewood, so I had set out just after lunch toward the north end of the island for a large fallen tree that I knew was dry and would burn strong. I had my saw slung over my shoulder, along with a sturdy piece of burlap to drag home the wood I collected.

While I walked, I watched the trees by the water to see if I could spot any of the black birds that sometimes roosted with their wings spread out to dry. They always reminded me of preachers with their black robes and arms spread out against the sky.

That's when I saw a flash of white through the trees, and I suddenly remembered Tiger telling me about the spirits that the Seminoles said lived in the forest. I didn't know what a spirit looked like, and I didn't want to find out. So I jumped off the trail and hid behind a thick slash pine. My eyes were glued to the trail up ahead, where I'd seen the white shape moving in the trees.

I tried telling myself that it was a real person, but I knew that wasn't true. Uncle Will had moved away the year before, up to Sand Point, and my parents had sent my little sister, Lillie, up north to a boarding school for girls. There weren't any people on the island except for me, Mama, and Papa. And those two were back at the house, where Papa was patching the roof yet again and Mama was tending to her blueberries in the garden.

Mama swore this was the year she was going to get blueberries in South Florida, no matter how many people told her that blueberries don't grow in South Florida because it gets too warm and there's no winter. Every time someone told her this, she would just smile and say that was between her and God.

Hiding behind the tree, I strained my ears and tried not to be too scared. After all, I was old enough that Papa took me out to hunt wild boar and had taught me how to use a sharp axe to clear land myself.

"HA!"

The shout came from directly behind me. I jumped in fright and yelled as I whirled around, the saw and the burlap flying out of my hands. Then I jumped in surprise.

Lillie was standing there, not five feet away, with a big grin on her face.

"How did … what the … what are you doing here?" I finally spluttered out. She had somehow crept up right behind me without so much as a whisper of sound. The only other person I knew who could do that was Tiger, but he was a Seminole, so it hardly counted.

Lillie did a little curtsey and ducked her head. "Nice to see you too, Mr. Charlie Pierce."

Then I got mad. "I'm serious, Lillie," I said. "You're supposed to be up at school. Are you on holiday?"

Lillie grinned. "Do I look like I'm on holiday?" In fact, she did not. Lillie was wearing boy's pants—which always drove Mama crazy—and a long-sleeved shirt. Her clothes were filthy, as if she'd been sleeping in a coal bin for a month, and her face was streaked with dirt. She had her hair woven into thick braids, and it looked as if she had tied it with a strip of bark she'd ripped off a tree. In all, I thought she looked more like a wild animal than my little sister.

"No," I finally said. "You don't look like you're on holiday." Then a new thought occurred to me. "You didn't run away from school, did you? Because if you did …"

But I stopped talking because I could tell from Lillie's grin that was exactly what she had done. Then her grin slipped a little, and she

13

looked worried. "I hated that school, Charlie. I told Papa that he might be able to make me go, but he couldn't make me stay."

"What was so bad about the school?" I asked. "Mama said it was the best girl's school in Florida."

Lillie snorted. "Maybe, as long as you like to needlepoint, sing from a hymnal, and dress up in ribbons and patent-leather shoes."

I laughed in spite of myself. Lillie was the last person on earth I could imagine dressed in ribbons and patent-leather shoes, and if you gave her a needle, she'd be more likely to bend it into a fishhook than attach thread to it.

"You wouldn't believe it!" Lillie continued. "We had one whole class where they made us walk with books balanced on our heads! 'Cause they said that would turn us into young ladies of distinction." Lillie stopped and spit impressively into the trees. "So much for young ladies of distinction."

I shook my head. "But I still don't get it. How'd you get home? Did Uncle Will go pick you up?"

"No!" Lillie said indignantly. "I walked."

Now I was really shocked. It had taken Papa two weeks to get Lillie the 250 miles north to Palatka, where the school was located. It was a complicated trip because Papa and Lillie had to sail up Lake Worth, travel through the woods to the Jupiter Inlet, go north up the Indian River on Captain Brevard's steamboat, and then north up the St. John's River to Palatka. "You walked?" I repeated, stunned.

"Sure," Lillie said, looking pretty smug. "It was no big deal. Look at this." She pulled out a bundle from her shirt and untied it. It was filled with grits. "I nicked this from the school kitchen on the way out. Two pounds of grits. I figured that's how much I'd need to eat on the way back. But I didn't even need any of it at all."

"So what'd you eat?" I asked.

"Charlie," Lillie said, "if you paid even a little attention, you wouldn't have to ask me that question. You can live off the land here in Florida for your whole life. You'd never have to buy another piece of food or drink of water. You've just got to know where to look."

I'll admit it: I was impressed. I didn't know anybody else who could make it 250 miles through the wilds of Florida on foot, except maybe Tiger. There's no way I would have tried such a foolish thing. But here was my little sister, who had done it all by herself with food to spare.

"So you think Papa will be mad?" Lillie asked, looking anxiously past me, down the trail and back toward our house.

"Are you kidding?" I said. "He's going to flip his hat over this." The truth was, Papa had been

16

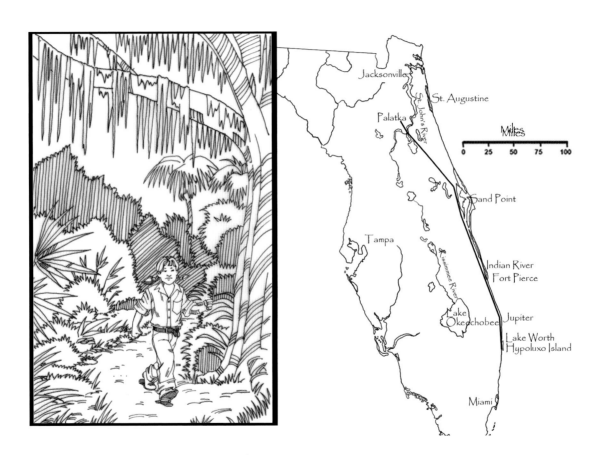

Jacksonville

St. Augustine

Palatka

St. John's River

Sand Point

Tampa

Kissimmee River

Indian River
Fort Pierce

Lake
Okeechobee

Jupiter

Lake Worth
Hypoluxo Island

Miami

Miles

0   25   50   75   100

looking distracted and worried lately. Something was bothering my parents, but they wouldn't say what it was. This wasn't going to help.

"Well, I'm not going back to school," Lillie said, her face hardening. "No matter what."

I sighed. The firewood didn't matter anymore. There was going to be plenty of fireworks around the house tonight without striking any flint. "C'mon, Lillie," I said. "We'd better head back to the house."

But just before I turned to leave, she grabbed my hand, and I could see how worried she was. That was just like Lillie. She could be as stubborn as an ox, but she hated letting people down or hurting anything. She had the biggest heart of almost anyone I knew, no matter how tough she acted on the outside.

"You understand, don't you, Charlie?" she asked. "You're not mad at me, right?"

I shook my head. "No," I said. "I understand. Now let's just hope Mama and Papa feel the same way."

But I was pretty sure they wouldn't.

Chapter Two

Papa's Secret

When Lillie and I walked from the woods into the clearing, Papa looked up from his hammering on the roof and Mama stood up in the garden patch. Then followed the longest minute of silence I could remember while they stared at Lillie.

I knew Lillie was scared, but she wasn't about to let it show, so she dropped my hand and stared back defiantly. When Mama came bustling over, the first thing Lillie said was, "I'm home for good, Mama."

Mama stared at Lillie with a hard look. Behind us, Papa clambered down from the roof and hastened over. I could see that Papa was worried — he often said that Mama and Lillie were cut from the same cloth, which really meant they were both stubborn as mules.

"Lillie, if I didn't know better, I'd say you were a ghost Charlie brought back from the woods," Papa called as he hurried over. "Why are you so dirty, girl? What's going on? Why aren't you at school?"

"'Cause I'm not going to that school no more."

"Any more," Mama grated, correcting Lillie's English. "You know perfectly well that it's 'any more.'"

"Did you run away from school?" Papa asked incredulously.

"Yep," Lillie said.

"But how did you get home?"

"I walked," Lillie said.

Mama gasped. "You walked! Do you have any idea how dangerous, how fool-headed that was, for a little girl to walk through the forest…"

"I'm not afraid of the woods," Lillie said, her voice rising to match Mama's.

"OK, OK," Papa said, holding his hands out. "We better head inside and get to the bottom of this. C'mon, Lillie."

The rest of the afternoon was one long argument. Mama was as mad as I'd ever seen her. She was so mad that she barely even said a word, and every time she started to talk, Papa hurried to cut her off before she could get up a good head of steam. And Lillie wasn't helping much.

It almost seemed as if she was trying to pick a fight with Mama because every chance she got, she declared that she'd rather live in the woods and grub for her own food than dress up in bows and buckled shoes.

Papa tried to lecture Lillie, but I actually felt a little sorry for him, stuck as he was between Mama and Lillie. It was a no-win situation, and he looked more miserable than angry.

Finally, Lillie was sent to bed before it was fully dark, and Mama and Papa sat tight-lipped and frowning, so I went outside to see if I could find any ripe huckleberries. Huckleberries are small, round berries that look a little like blueberries, but in my opinion taste much better. They are sweet and sometimes a little tart. Before Lillie went away, she used to collect huckleberries by the basketful for Mama to make into jam and pies. But since Lillie had been gone, Mama hadn't done any cooking with huckleberries because she spent all her time fooling with her blueberries.

I spent as long as I could searching out the best huckleberries while also eating my fill. I kept an alert ear out for bears—it wasn't uncommon to find black bears on the island looking for ripe huckleberries also. Lillie even used to feed the bears, right up until Papa threatened to shoot any that got too close to the house or too used to humans.

Finally, I walked slowly back to the house with heavy feet. I wasn't looking forward to waking up the next morning. I knew that if Mama had her way, they would pack Lillie back off to school the very next morning. I could already guess what Lillie would say about that.

Night was falling as I neared the house, and the emerging moon cast shadows through the banyan and sabal palms that grew up to our clearing. The moonlight glinted off the dark water of Lake Worth, and a light breeze rattled the fresh palm fronds that Papa had nailed on the roof that afternoon. The sound must have covered my footsteps because I was sure that Mama and Papa didn't mean for me to hear them talking.

"So you mean to just let her stay?" Mama was saying angrily. They were sitting in the main room, and the front door was open to let in the breeze. I could hear them just as if I was sitting in the room with them.

"Well, yes, I guess I do," Papa said. "You heard what she said, and you know she means it. How many other little girls—how many other people—do you know who could do what she did? She made it all that way down the state with no gun, no flint, no water, no nothing, and she looked like she'd just come in from a Sunday stroll—"

"Excepting that she was filthy!" Mama interrupted. "You almost sound proud of her! It isn't proper for a young lady to act in that way! I know this is a wild place, so we must choose the kind of society we make here…"

"Do we really choose, though?" Papa said. "Lillie's been this way since she was born. I don't know how much choice there is in the matter."

There was a long silence, and I could just picture Mama sitting with her hands drawn up in her lap and her mouth in a tight line. Mama wasn't a hard person — not at all. But she had very specific ideas on how we should be educated — especially Lillie — and that included history, literature, music, language, and geography lessons. Where Lillie was concerned, it didn't include tracking animals and woodlore. Mama had come from moneyed people up North, in Chicago, and she often said the land might be wild, but we didn't have to be.

"So your mind is made up," Mama said. "But that leaves just one question. What about the tuition money? You heard what the headmaster said. There are no refunds for students who leave school early. We already paid for her education. So we'll just lose all that money. You know what that means. Unless one of your land investments pays off, and sooner than later, we might have to sell this island."

I heard Papa sigh, and my mind suddenly whirled with questions. A few years before, a hurricane had come, and I'd found a trunk full of Spanish gold half buried on the beach. Papa and Uncle Will had dragged the trunk back to Hypoluxo Island and buried it under the big banyan tree out front and agreed to split the money. They dug it up every so often, whenever we needed money. That included the day Uncle Will bought his sailboat, the *Magellan*, and moved away, and the day that Lillie went off to school. I'd always thought there was enough gold in that chest to last a lifetime. Could it really be gone?

Finally, after a long silence, Papa said, "I know the situation, but Lillie being home doesn't change it any. It was going to be the same either way. We knew that all along."

"So it's OK to just throw that money away to the wind?" Mama asked.

"No, I'm not saying that!" Papa answered in an agitated voice. "I'm just saying that one thing doesn't necessarily connect with the other. And that I don't think money is a good enough reason to send Lillie back! We'll figure something out. We're not selling!"

Mama went silent as a bad feeling settled into the pit of my stomach. Could it be true? I knew that land speculators were moving into this area. They were buying up big pieces of swampland and forestland. Papa, too, had made some land investments. But he couldn't afford the better farmland on the western shore of the lake, where a few men were talking about growing citrus and pineapples. Instead, Papa had bought on the low barrier islands to the east. I knew most people thought it was foolish to buy sandy islands so close to the ocean. Nothing grew there, and we'd already seen what a hurricane could do. But this was the first I heard that

25

we might have to move and that my parents needed money.

I resolved right then not to say anything to Lillie. If she knew they had spent the last of the Spanish gold on her schooling, and that her running away meant it was wasted, she would never forgive herself.

But like Papa said, that didn't solve the real problem: were we really going to lose our beloved island?

Chapter Three

A Stranger Visits

Papa woke me up at first light that next morning. He looked tired, as if he hadn't slept much. "C'mon, Charlie," he said. "That wood won't collect itself."

In a few minutes, we had eaten some cold Indian pumpkin and salt pork and were heading back into the forest with the two-man saw. I was boiling with questions to ask Papa, but I couldn't let him know I had eavesdropped the night before. Instead, I said, "Are you going to send Lillie back to school?"

Papa glanced at me and shook his head. "I don't want to take the chance that she'll run away again. Next time, she might not get so lucky on the way home."

I didn't have anything to say to that, so I just helped Papa find a downed tree. We cut the trunk into big sections and loaded them onto a makeshift sled so we could drag them home to split into firewood. By the time we got back, dragging the heavy load of wood, it was already midmorning, and we were both dripping with sweat and swatting away clouds of black flies.

Back at home, a thin column of smoke was rising from the brick chimney. Mama was cooking breakfast, and my stomach growled.

But Papa stopped suddenly as we emerged from the woods and stared at our boat landing. A small skiff, with a single droopy sail, was heading for our dock. It was manned by a lone man with wild hair and a bristly beard that almost touched his chest. When he saw us, he hailed and yelled, "Hello! This your island? Are you the Pierces?"

"Morning, stranger," Papa called back, mopping his face and hurrying down to the landing. I saw Mama appear in the doorway of our house, wiping her hands on her apron. Lillie instantly appeared in the doorway and tried to scoot around Mama, but Mama shooed her back inside. We didn't get many strangers visiting our island.

In a minute, Papa had tied the skiff to the dock, and the stranger was stepping from his boat onto the landing. It wasn't just his hair and beard that were wild — he looked as if he hadn't bathed in months, and the skin of his face was tanned a deep brown and wrinkled.

"I'm John Samuelson," he said, sticking his hand out. "I don't mean to intrude on your family, but I'm sailing north to Sand Point, up from way down past Miami, and, well, I was hoping

you could spare a little something to eat. I'd be happy to pay you, but I've been sailing all night, and I'm powerfully sick of dried fowl. You folks on this lovely island are just about the only people anywhere around here."

Papa rocked back on his heels while I wandered over for a closer look. Papa always said you can tell a man's character from his eyes, but it was nearly impossible to see John Samuelson's eyes as they were hidden in deep wrinkles under his bushy eyebrows. I looked in his boat and saw that it was packed tight with wooden crates, all the way past the gunwales. But whatever he was carrying must have been pretty light—the boat was still riding high up in the water. He had a rifle sitting next to the tiller, close enough that he could reach it while still sailing.

Papa must have decided that Mr. Samuelson wasn't dangerous, because he shook his hand and said, "Sure. Come on up. Looks like you're just in time for breakfast."

Mr. Samuelson followed us to the house. When he walked inside, I saw him look up and smile under his rough beard. He saw me watching him, and I think he winked at me, but I wasn't sure. Then he said, "Nice house you've got here. It's been a long time since I had a roof over my head."

Soon he was seated at our kitchen table, along with Papa and Lillie and me, while Mama mashed up more pumpkin, mixed up batter for biscuits to fry in bacon grease, and set a skillet of bacon on the stove.

"So," Papa said, "what business do you have in Sand Point? My brother-in-law, Will, lives up there. He says it's turning into a regular town, with a main street and everything."

Mr. Samuelson shrugged. "I wouldn't know. I haven't seen anything like a town in months. Thank you, ma'am," he said as Mama set a cup of coffee in front of him. He smelled it deeply and smiled. "Fresh coffee is one of life's great pleasures. As for Sand Point, I'm heading up there to trade plumes."

"Plumes?" said Papa. "You mean bird plumes?"

"Yessir," Mr. Samuelson said. "Haven't you heard? Plumes is the new gold."

But Papa just looked blankly at Mr. Samuelson, and I sat trying to figure out why bird feathers would be the new gold. As far as I knew, the only thing bird feathers were good for was stuffing pillows and making me sneeze at night.

Mr. Samuelson laughed and sipped at his coffee. "You have no idea what I'm talking about, do you?"

Papa shook his head, and I could see he was getting aggravated. "No, I guess I don't."

"Look here." Mr. Samuelson pulled a yellowed page from inside his coat and unfolded it. The page had been creased many times over, and it looked as if he'd been carrying it through all kinds of weather for a long time. He put one thick finger on the page, pushed it toward us, and said, "See?"

31

We all crowded around and looked. The page was an advertisement from a magazine. "FINE LADIES' HATS!" it proclaimed. Then it showed pictures of ladies in long hoopskirted dresses wearing giant hats that were decorated with bird feathers.

"Hats?" Mama said. "They're putting plumes on hats now?" We all knew that Mama had a special place in her heart for birds. Of all her books, one of her favorites was an old volume called *Birds of America*, by a painter named John James Audubon. Mama sometimes read aloud from the passages, and I suspected this was where Lillie first got her love of animals—birds were one thing she and Mama could agree on.

"Indeed, ma'am, they are decorating hats with plumes now," Mr. Samuelson said. "You can't turn around in Manhattan without nearly losing an eye to some feathered hat. But they need plumes, and they're willing to pay top dollar for 'em."

"Well I'll be," mused Papa.

"You know," Mr. Samuelson said, leaning back and leaving the page on the table. Lillie was still studying it, probably to see whether she recognized the kinds of birds the feathers came from. No doubt she did. I thought I even recognized a heron feather—and herons and cormorants were about the only birds I knew.

"You should give it a try," Mr. Samuelson said to Papa. "Plume hunting, that is. This whole place is thick with birds."

This was true. Florida teemed with great flocks of birds in every color. We saw many birds on the island, wading in the shallows or roosting in the trees.

"No thanks," Papa laughed. "We've got plenty to do around here without going feather collecting."

"Really?" Mr. Samuelson said. "What if I told you that I knew a place where a man could make $1,000 in a single week?"

The smile slipped from Papa's face, and even Mama muttered in surprise. Mr. Samuelson had their attention now, and he seemed to be enjoying himself. I wasn't sure whether I liked him after all, plumes or no plumes.

"Yep," Mr. Samuelson said. "You know what a rookery is?"

"It's a place where birds nest," Lillie piped up immediately. Mr. Samuelson glanced at her and smiled indulgently. "That's right," he said. "A place where birds nest. Well, let me tell you, if you find the right rookery, it's like money falling from the sky."

"There's rookeries all over around here," Lillie said.

"Not like the rookeries I've seen," Mr. Samuelson said, and he leaned forward. "If you go south from here far enough, you hit a place where there's nothing but sawgrass and swamp. The Indians call it *Pa-Hay-Okee*. But white men don't go there because of the malaria and yellow fever. And it's infested with gators and poisonous snakes of all kinds. Most men who venture in there never come out again."

I knew about *Pa-Hay-Okee* from Tiger — the Seminoles had lived around the great swamp since anyone could remember. The word *Pa-Hay-Okee* meant "grassy water," and Tiger said he'd explored the swamp. Later, white men would call it the Everglades. Tiger said it went as far as you could see, and that not even the Seminoles knew everything about the great swamp.

"Well," Samuelson continued, "no white man goes there excepting me, that is. I'm just now coming back from six months up in the swamp, and the only reason I'm coming back at all is because I can't put any more plumes in my boat and I ran out of bullets. But," he paused dramatically, "you can bet I'll be back."

"Oh? And why is that?" Papa said. I could tell from his tone of voice that he wasn't much impressed with John Samuelson, but Samuelson didn't seem to notice.

"Because," Samuelson gloated, "I found me a secret place. A place better'n an Incan city full of gold."

"Really?" Papa asked skeptically.

"Yessir I did. If you don't believe me, just look at this." Again Samuelson put his hand in his jacket, but this time he withdrew a singular white feather. It was pure white and shone in the weak morning light. "You know what this is?" Samuelson asked Lillie.

She shook her head.

"Snowy egret," Samuelson said. "These are the finest plumes in the world. You can get forty dollars for a single ounce of these feathers. Now imagine a place with so many thousands of birds that they fill the sky for ten heartbeats as they fly overhead."

He stopped and waited while we pictured the sky filled with brilliant white birds like so much flying money. I looked at Papa. Surely he must have been thinking the same thing I was thinking. But I couldn't read the expression on his face as he looked at the white feather shining in Samuelson's hand.

Samuelson continued. "That's what I found. The biggest snowy egret rookery in the world. And I'm probably the only man alive who knows where it is." I think he might have been smirking underneath his beard, as if he was waiting for Papa or someone else to start begging him for the location of this rookery.

But Papa just gave him a thin smile and said, "Plume hunting. Doesn't that just beat all?"

I couldn't believe it. It was the first time in my life that I thought Papa was making a huge mistake. Just at the very moment we needed money, a man had shown up on our doorstep

with an easy way to make a fortune. It was almost as easy as finding a chest of gold on the beach. But Papa didn't seem interested at all! I was squirming in my chair so badly that Mama finally shot me a "calm down" look as she served breakfast.

John Samuelson didn't stick around for too long after he ate. He thanked us and tried to give Papa a quarter for breakfast, but Papa wouldn't take the money. Then Samuelson headed back for his boat. I quickly offered to help cast off his ropes and jogged alongside him.

As soon as we were away from the house, I said, "So where is this place? This rookery?"

Samuelson glanced down at me, and his booming laughter suddenly shattered the quiet morning. "The boy has ambitions!" he said.

"C'mon," I said, glancing back at the house. "I just want to know…"

But Samuelson stopped on the dock and fixed me with a piercing glare. "You and every other scoundrel," Samuelson said. "Why don't you ask for my boat? Or my watch?" He chuckled, and I decided I didn't like him in the least. "No," Samuelson said. "After I sell these skins here, I'm going for it myself. And I'll be bringing a bigger boat."

Then he looked up over my shoulder as Papa joined us on the dock. "Thank you kindly for breakfast," John Samuelson said, and he winked at me while I glared at him.

"You're welcome," Papa said. "A good day to sail. You've got a fair wind."

Samuelson grinned beneath his wild beard. "Indeed I do. You could even say the wind is at my back." He boomed out another jolt of laughter. "Thank the missus for me, for breakfast." He inclined his head toward me. "And keep a watch on this one, eh? From the look of him, his eyes are bigger than his belly."

Papa didn't bother to answer but just looked evenly at John Samuelson.

In another moment, Samuelson was tacking out into the lake and heading north. I kept waiting for Papa to say something about plume hunting or ask me what Samuelson had meant, but he never did. Instead, he just said, "C'mon now, Charlie, let's finish up with that wood."

Chapter Four

For Sale!

After Samuelson left, I kept waiting for Papa to say something about plume hunting. It seemed like the easiest way in the world to make money, if we needed money. There were enough birds in the sky to fill a thousand boats with feathers, and if New Yorkers wanted to pay top dollar for them, then I couldn't see why we shouldn't oblige those folks.

But Papa never said anything, and in fact he seemed to get more distracted as the days went by. Finally, I found out why.

One day another man visited our island. This man was wearing a suit with a vest and pocket watch on a chain. He carried a folder wrapped in twine and wore leather shoes that were made for city streets, not muddy trails. When he stepped from the boat, he nearly fell off the dock, and Papa had to grab his arm quick to keep him from plunging into the lake's dark waters. The man said his name was William H. Gleason, broker and sales agent, and Papa didn't look any too happy to see him.

Papa and Gleason spent that whole day going over our island, carefully inspecting the clearing where we lived and the forest that covered the rest of the island. Mr. Gleason seemed impressed, which made sense because everybody knew we had the most beautiful island anywhere around.

While they were looking, Mama was distracted and short-tempered, and even Lillie figured out something serious was going on and avoided Mama. Finally Gleason left, and Papa stood on the dock for a long time, watching the water and looking at the sky.

That night at dinner, Papa made a simple announcement that dropped on us like a cold stone: "We're putting the island up for sale."

Before anybody could say another word, Lillie jumped up and nearly tipped her plate over. "Papa, no!" she said. "Why would you sell the island?"

"Well, Lillie…" Papa started, but Lillie just talked right over him. "I don't want to sell the island! Why would you sell the island? I don't want to live nowhere else…"

"Lillie!" Mama suddenly yelled, and Lillie stopped talking. "You sit down, young lady! And don't raise your voice to your Papa like that! This was a hard enough decision to make, but we've made it."

All the air seemed to go out of Lillie, and she collapsed back into her chair. Her eyes were already filling with tears. "Why?" she started to whine. "But Papa…"

"Now Lillie," Papa said sadly, "I know it's hard to understand, but this island is getting too expensive for us to keep. There's a thing called property taxes, and as long as more people keep moving in, them property taxes keep going up. And … well, we just don't need this much land. Mr. Gleason, who was here today, he said this island would be worth quite a lot because it's on freshwater. So once we sell it, we'll be able to get a smaller, more manageable plot somewhere else."

Lillie was crying now, and Papa looked miserable. She opened her mouth to say something else, but Mama cut her off: "No more com-plaining, Lillie." There was something steely and hard in Mama's voice, and for the first time in my life, I saw Lillie struck speechless. She snapped her mouth shut with an audible POP! and stared at Mama for a long minute, then her face finally crumpled and she ran away from the table.

"Papa?" I said in the silence that followed. They turned to me, and I finally asked the question that had been on my mind since John Samuelson visited: "If we need money, how come we don't do what John Samuelson said? You heard what he said about the rookeries, right? Why don't we go plume hunting?"

Papa sighed and shook his head. He thought for a long minute before he answered. "I wondered how long it would take you to get around to that. I saw that Mr. Samuelson's stories gripped your imagination. But Charlie, here's the thing about easy money. There's always strings attached. Killing birds is no way to make an honest living. It's a rough business full of rough men who wouldn't think anything of putting a bullet in you just for some money. And make no mistake about it: the greed of men knows no bounds. No matter how many birds there are now, there aren't enough to satisfy the thirst for money that afflicts some men. I don't want my family to get caught between men like John Samuelson and their money, killing things we don't need to kill to live. It's not the way I want to raise a family."

"But…"

"No, Charlie," Papa said. "We'll find a way to provide for ourselves and still hold our heads up high. That's the Pierce way."

I knew from his tone of voice that there was no arguing with Papa, but I sure didn't agree with him. His reasoning sounded as thin as a blade of sawgrass, and I couldn't help my feelings as I prepared for bed that evening. I was mad at Papa for turning his back on a way to save the island, I was mad at Lillie for running away from school and wasting all the money that could have saved our island, and I was even a little mad at Mr. Gleason for his shiny leather shoes and shiny watch.

And I didn't agree with Papa about the nature of the plume hunters. I'd heard plenty of times that if a person wanted to make his way in the world, he had to go out and make opportunity. It was the American way. So what was hunting plumes but the American way?

Lying there in bed, stewing in anger, I decided to make some opportunities for myself. If Papa wasn't going to find John Samuelson's secret snowy egret rookery, then I would.

44

Chapter Five

Friends to the Rescue

I might have disagreed with Papa about plume hunting, but he was right about one thing: there sure were a lot of new people moving into the area. The shores of Lake Worth were slowly being cleared for new homesteads, and a few farmers were planting large farms.

I even noticed that game was becoming harder to find. We had to go deeper into the big pine forests to find wild turkey, hog, deer, and rabbit for the table. There was a time when we barely had to step off the front porch to find everything we needed.

But having new neighbors wasn't all bad. Right in the middle of our troubles, a new family called the Bradley family bought a plot of land on the west side of the lake just north of our island. Just as we did with all our new neighbors, Papa offered to help them clear the homestead and build a house, and that's how I met my best friends, Guy and Louis Bradley.

Guy was my age, and Louis was two years younger. I liked them right away. When I started planning my expedition to go after those snowy egrets, I knew just who I wanted to come along with me. Guy was a crack shot and a good sailor, and Louis could catch just about any fish that swam in either fresh or salt water. Better still, they never stopped talking about the famous Lewis and Clark expedition, where Meriwether Lewis and William Clark made it all the way from Pittsburgh to the Pacific Ocean and back. I figured Guy and Louis would jump at the chance to make a Great Plume Bird Expedition with me into the Everglades.

That left just one more boy I hoped would come along: my old friend Tiger. Fortunately, I knew Tiger made an annual hunting trip down the coast, right past Hypoluxo Island, so I convinced Guy and Louis to come with me, and we went off to find Tiger. They were surprised at first, but I explained that a lot of Seminole boys traveled alone to hunt and trade for themselves.

It took some good luck, but fortunately I knew all of Tiger's favorite camping places on the barrier islands, and it didn't take long before we saw a thin plume of smoke and found Tiger and his canoe at a small camp by the water. We hailed him, and Tiger jumped up and waved at us.

After introductions, the four of us made the short hike to the ocean and found a place to sit in the shade of a stand of sea grape trees and watch the waves foam across the white

sand. After we all settled in, I said, "So, boys, I've got an adventure for you, if you're interested."

"An adventure?" Guy said. "What kind of adventure?"

"Do we get to fish?" Louis said.

"Definitely," I said, "and more besides." Then I explained all about John Samuelson and my idea of a Great Plume Bird Expedition. I especially focused on how much money we could make. I said the Bradley brothers could likely buy their very own sailboat, and Tiger could get his village just about anything he wanted.

"And if you think about it," I finished, "we'll be just like real explorers, just like Lewis and Clark. We'll have to go into the big swamp of Pa-Hay-Okee. What do you think?"

"Our parents'll never let us go off like that," Louis said. "Pa'd whip us good."

"Maybe," I agreed. "But what if you came back with a sackful of money?"

"I dunno…" Louis said uncertainly.

Then Guy cut in, "You say we'd actually go into Pa-Hay-Okee? I thought only the Indians went in there. I didn't think white men went into the swamp."

"Well then we'd be the first," I said. "Except Tiger. You've been there before, right?"

Tiger nodded. "Yes. My people know Pa-Hay-Okee."

"See?" I said. "If Tiger comes, we'll be with a real Seminole who's been there before. And you'll come along, right, Tiger?"

He shrugged. "Where is rookery?" he asked. "Pa-Hay-Okee very large. You know where rookery is?"

"Well not exactly," I said. "But look." I unfolded a map that I had brought from home. It showed the coast of Florida from north of our island all the way down to Miami. "Samuelson came up from Miami, so I figure that means he came down the Miami River, right? We could sail south to Biscayne Bay, then go up the Miami River." I traced my finger along the route until it faded into nothing. "We'll end up here."

"Yes, but where is rookery in there?" Tiger said, wiping his hand across the big blank spot on the map where the Everglades was.

"I don't know in particular," I answered. "But there can't be too many big rookeries full of snowy egrets. We'll just look until we find it."

Tiger shook his head a little. "I don't know, Charlie. Pa-Hay-Okee is very wild. Even Seminoles don't know everywhere."

"I know," I said. "But that means Samuelson couldn't have gone very far, right? He was probably just on the edge. You probably know the swamp better'n he does."

When Tiger didn't answer, I said, "You'll come, right, Tiger? You're the only one who's been there before."

Finally, Tiger shrugged. "Yes. I come."

I sighed in relief.

"One more question," Guy said. "You said we were gonna sail down there? How can we do that?"

"That'll be the easy part," I answered. "My Uncle Will…"

"Shh!" Tiger suddenly hissed, and we immediately fell silent. He cupped his hand at his ear like we should listen, but I couldn't hear anything except waves on the beach. Still, I knew better than to ignore Tiger's warning. These woods were full of bears and even panthers. I wished I'd brought along my rifle.

Suddenly Tiger jumped up and ran back over the dune. The three of us leaped up and followed him. We found Tiger crouching on the ground at the edge of the slash pines, where the sand was covered with pine needles.

"Look," he said, pointing down.

There was a little depression in the sand. "What is it? Bear? Panther?"

"No," said Tiger. "Human."

We strained our eyes into the forest, but there wasn't anything to see. If someone had been listening to us, he was gone now, leaving only a footprint in the sand.

Chapter Six

On Our Own

We started to plan our secret expedition right away, which meant provisioning ourselves for a long hunting trip. I packed as much food and supplies as I could into waterproof containers and hid the containers all over the island. The Bradley brothers were doing the same thing at their house.

We figured we'd be gone for at least a few weeks, so we packed plenty of dry food, including cornmeal for grits, flour and baking powder for biscuits, dried pork, cans of beans, jars of pickled vegetables, and I even managed to find a few jars of Mama's huckleberry jam.

Remembering what John Samuelson said about running out of bullets, we'd also need a lot of ammunition. I figured this would be the hardest part because both my Papa and the Bradleys' Pa kept their ammunition in locked cabinets. They would know right away if any went missing.

But then we fell onto a good piece of luck: Papa said he and Mr. Bradley had some work to do and would me and Guy and Louis be willing to run up to the Brelsfords' store and buy some supplies?

I readily agreed, so Guy, Louis, and I sailed up Lake Worth to the Brelsfords' general store. The store was run by two brothers, E. M. and Doc Brelsford. They had a post office at the store, and they knew us pretty well from our trips up to collect the mail and Mama's magazines. They called their post office "Palm Beach." Later on, the whole area would use that same name. It turned out that the Brelsfords knew how to pick a nice piece of property. Some years later, their small store would be torn down by a rich oil tycoon named Henry Flagler, who built a grand home called Whitehall on the site.

The Brelsfords' general store wasn't very big, and they knew most every family in the area, which meant they knew what we usually needed. When I handed over our order, Doc Brelsford whistled under his breath and said, "Shoot, you boys planning on taking on an army with all this ammunition?"

I tried to laugh so he wouldn't get suspicious. "No, sir. Just a hunting trip."

"I'll say." Doc filled our order for birdshot, plus larger slugs for game like bears and hogs, in addition to Papa's order for kerosene, vinegar, cocoa, onions, and fish hooks.

On the way back, I tried not to feel too guilty about charging so much ammunition to our account. But then I thought about how much money we'd make, and I promised I'd pay Papa back for everything, plus give him all the extra money we were going to make from the plumes.

The last thing we needed was a boat, but I knew just where we could find the perfect boat. Before my Uncle Will had moved up to Sand Point, he'd used some of his Spanish gold to buy a twenty-eight-foot sailboat with a seven-foot beam and a little covered cabin. He used it to run supplies and people up and down the east coast of Florida, from Jacksonville to Key West. He'd named it the *Magellan*, after the great Portuguese navigator of the early 1500s who was the first person to sail around the world.

When Uncle Will wasn't using the *Magellan*, he kept it tied up near his old cabin on the north end of Hypoluxo Island — which is where it was right then.

I knew taking Uncle Will's boat could land me in serious trouble, even worse than the ammunition. But again, I promised myself that, just as with Papa, I'd pay for it myself if anything happened to the *Magellan*. The way I figured it, we'd have enough money to buy Uncle Will a whole new boat.

Still, as the night before the Great Plume Bird Expedition ticked away, I lay in bed awake and nervous. I'd never hidden such a big thing from Mama and Papa. Part of me knew that I'd been stealing food and supplies, and Mama would say that I'd stolen money buying all that ammunition. I could hear her voice in my head: "That's not how we raised you, Charlie. That's not the Pierce way."

But then I reminded myself why I was doing all this. It wasn't for me. I figured it would be different if I was sneaking away so I could do something selfish. But I wasn't. I was only doing something that needed to be done for the whole family, and wasn't that what Papa said it meant to be a man? To take care of your family?

Still, it didn't make sleep come any easier, so I sat up and wrote a short note to Mama and Papa explaining where I'd gone and why.

Finally, sometime before dawn, I slipped from my bed and tiptoed through the house as quiet as a shadow. When I passed Lillie's door, I stopped and almost checked on her. But then I decided the sound of the door might wake her up, so I went outside into the still night.

The last thing I did before I left was set a letter to Mama and Papa on the kitchen table:

Dear Mama & Papa,
I know you'll be surprised when you find my bed empty and this letter on the table. Don't worry. I didn't get ~~carryed~~ carried off by bears. Papa, I know you said you didn't want to plume hunt because it wasn't any way to make a living. But I'm not trying to make a

living. I just want to make enough money to save our island. Please don't worry about me. I know what I'm doing.

With Love,

Charlie

P.S.: Guy and Louis Bradley came along, too, and we took Uncle Will's boat. I figured no one was using it for the time being.

Outside, I walked up the trail toward Uncle Will's cabin. The island was still under the blanket of night, and the moon peeked through the pine trees and glittered off the water. The air smelled fresh and clean, and the ground was soft underfoot as I followed the path toward the water. I felt more than ever that I didn't want to leave our island. I loved this island.

When I reached the *Magellan*, the boat was riding low in the water because I'd already loaded all the supplies on board. I waded through the warm, shallow water, clambered aboard, cast off the lines, and set out alone. The dark water shushed alongside the boat, the shore was quiet, and I felt like the only person on the planet.

A great blue heron suddenly swooped by, its huge wings causing ripples over the dark water. I almost jumped right out of my skin, but then I laughed at myself a little. Spooked by a bird!

Just as I planned, it was still dark when I finally came within sight of the Bradleys' dock. I sailed on past and dropped anchor silently a little ways up the shore to wait for my friends. The eastern horizon was just beginning to lighten. Dawn was coming. I hoped Guy and Louis would hurry up and tried not to get nervous. I was sure that like everyone in these parts, their parents would be up with the first light of dawn.

I heard someone sneeze before I saw anybody, and my heart started pounding. I watched the shore anxiously, hoping we wouldn't be discovered before the expedition even started.

But it was only Guy and Louis, walking down the path toward the shore. I noticed that Louis had lashed his favorite fishing pole to his pack and smiled. Louis stifled another sneeze in his shirt as they waded out to the boat and climbed in. Pretty soon, Guy started coughing too.

"You better quiet down," I said, helping Guy aboard. "You're gonna wake up your whole house."

"Can't heb it," Guy said, sniffling.

"Me neeber," Louis added.

It turned out they'd both fallen ill two days before. It was rotten luck, but there was nothing we could do about it. It was now or never. So I hoisted the sail, and we headed north to the inlet to pick up Tiger.

We were treated to a beautiful sunrise, but the sailing was hard and took much longer than I expected. An easterly breeze was coming from the ocean, and we had to zigzag across the lake to make any progress.

It didn't help much that Guy and Louis were both so sick they couldn't do much besides sit and watch me handle the lines and tiller. Once I even caught Louis curled up on the floor of the boat, sleeping.

When we finally reached the inlet, we sailed close to the shore and kept our eyes peeled for Tiger. He was supposed to meet us, and I was anxious and ready to get on the ocean.

Finally, I saw my friend paddling out to us in his dugout canoe. He climbed aboard, and we lifted his canoe onto the *Magellan's* deck and lashed it down.

We were finally ready, and everybody was excited to get the Great Plume Bird Expedition officially started. Even Louis seemed to perk up a little bit as I pointed the bow of the *Magellan* for the narrow inlet and we headed for the Atlantic Ocean.

Chapter Seven

A Stowaway

We sailed out the inlet into the quickly rising sun and a decent surf, whipped up by the easterly wind. My friends held on and looked nervous while I took the tiller.

The *Magellan* plunged and crashed through the waves, sending great sprays of salt water over the bow, but I wasn't worried. The *Magellan* was a good boat, and I had sailed enough times on the Atlantic Ocean to respect its power.

As long as we didn't get stuck in the Gulf Stream, there wouldn't be any trouble. The Gulf Stream is a strong current of warm water that pushes north from the Gulf of Mexico. It's hard to sail south in the Gulf Stream because the fast-moving water travels north and can push you off course.

Personally, I thought Louis wouldn't mind getting stuck in the Gulf Stream, which is famous for its fishing. Uncle Will, Papa, and I had fished the Gulf Stream last spring and caught tuna and sail fish and even one huge fish that was bigger than Papa. Uncle Will called it a blue marlin.

But on this day, I kept us within sight of the wild coastline and made good time as the wind shifted to the west. I figured we could run down to the Hillsboro River Inlet, some forty miles away, and arrive around nightfall. We planned to spend the night there and then head inland and start looking for birds.

The first day passed well. Tiger helped me steer the tiller when my hand got tired of fighting waves, and Guy and Louis sneezed every time they got soaked with salt spray. We didn't see any other boats. The only other person we saw was the keeper at the Orange Grove House,

Stephen Andrews, who waved at us as we passed. For lunch, we had dried salt beef and a can of beans on the boat.

Finally, with the sun long past its overhead mark, we neared the mouth of the Hillsboro River. The wind had been slacking off all afternoon, so the swells weren't bad as we approached the inlet. Guy appeared next to the tiller and eyed the narrow inlet. There were waves breaking to either side, and the mouth of the river looked mighty narrow.

"You think we can make it through there?" he asked.

I nodded. "Hope so. We sure don't want to run aground."

I told Tiger to drop the jib, and we half-lowered the main sail to slow us down. The last thing I wanted to do was come at the inlet too fast and beach the *Magellan*. The tide was coming in, so I thought as long as we stayed near the center of the inlet, we would make it.

My friends sat on the bow while we rode the last of the big waves in toward the inlet. The water got choppy and brown where the darker water from the river mixed with the blue ocean water, and I realized I was holding my breath as we passed the first sand dunes.

Don't ground, don't ground, don't ground, I thought.

But the *Magellan* sailed smoothly into the inlet and into the river. Guy looked back at me and grinned, and I let my breath out in a big whoosh. We had made the first part of our journey.

"Anchors away!" I sang out happily. I grinned as Tiger leaped down and heaved the anchor overboard with a splash.

We were planning to spend the night on the river, then sail upriver to a place called Lettuce Lake to see if we could find a rookery and get a few birds. Everything was going perfectly, that is until I opened the tiny door to the boat's cabin and a voice from inside said, "Ow!"

I jumped back and yelled, "Hey!"

Tiger jumped up toward the cabin, a look of alarm on his face, and Guy yelled, "What is it?!"

Tiger and Guy looked at me in alarm, then at the cabin door, as if they expected a full-grown alligator to climb out of the cabin. But I knew it wasn't an alligator. It was worse.

"Oh no," I mumbled as I went back to the cabin and pushed aside a few crates. Then the voice yelled, "Fine! I'm coming out! I'm coming out!"

And we all watched in amazement as my little sister, Lillie, dragged herself out from the pile of provisions and emerged from the cabin, blinking a little and looking at me defiantly. I suddenly knew who had been eavesdropping on us that day on the beach dune.

"What are you doing!" I yelled at her. I was furious.

"You're going plume hunting in the big swamp," Lillie said. "I'm coming."

"Oh no you're not," I said. "No way."

"Yeah, this isn't a trip for girls," Guy added.

Lillie glared at Guy. "Is too. Anyway, you can't stop me. I'm coming."

"Lillie," I said, "Mama and Papa would lose their minds with worry…"

"I doubt it," Lillie said. "Mama's always mad at me now anyway, and Papa's just trying to sell the island. Anyway, you're going. So I'm going."

"But…" I started.

"Fine," Lillie said in a breezy voice. "Then take me home." She looked at me smugly.

I sighed. She had me, and she knew it. If we took her home, the whole trip would be ruined, and we'd probably never have a chance again. I looked at Tiger.

Guy and Louis groaned—they already knew how annoying Lillie could be. She often followed us around on the island, imitating birdcalls just to drive us crazy. Only Tiger grinned. He'd always liked Lillie.

I held my hands up. "Fine," I said. "You win. But just don't do anything stupid and get hurt, OK? Mama and Papa would never forgive me."

Lillie laughed out loud. "That's funny, Charlie! You looked and sounded just like Papa right then!"

"Oh shush," I growled, but I was secretly a little pleased.

Now that we were five instead of four, we settled into a dinner of cold salted pork, water, and even a jar of pickled vegetables. I thought Mama would probably fall over if she knew we were eating vegetables without being told to, but I saw Louis dump most of his overboard when he thought no one was looking. I looked into the water and saw a bunch of little fish swarming around the green beans and carrots.

As night fell, we rode at anchor and listened to the wildlife come out in the jungle around us. The river was a wild, untamed place. The banks were overrun with mangrove and thick vines, and the trees were covered with Spanish moss.

Birdcalls echoed through the forest. Swarms of mosquitoes seemed to rise from the water itself and buzz all around us.

The last thing I thought before I went to sleep was that, as annoying as Lillie was, she probably had just as much right to go plume hunting as I did—and she could probably survive better in the wild than me anyway.

But still, who wants to go on an adventure with his little sister?

Chapter Eight

Lettuce Lake

We woke up with the first light. The birds in the trees were squawking, and all the animals seemed very animated. The strong eastern wind from the day before must have blown in a heat wave because the air was already growing hot. I scratched at the mosquito bites already covering my arms and figured we'd be sweating all day.

"So where are we going anyway?" Lillie asked as the other boys woke up and we gathered on the deck to eat.

"Lettuce Lake," I answered. "Up Cypress Creek."

"What's there?" Lillie asked.

"Birds," I said. I was still annoyed with her for stowing away, and here she was acting like this was a great big adventure and we'd almost begged her to come along.

"So you're gonna shoot 'em when you find 'em?" she asked.

"That's the general plan," I said.

"How many you think you'll find?" she asked.

"As many as we can," Guy said, and Louis nodded. "They're worth a fortune, you know."

"Not all of them," Lillie said. "How are you going to miss the birds that aren't worth as much?"

Guy looked at me and rolled his eyes. "Can you stop pestering?" I said. "That's not how you plume hunt, Lillie. You just blast as many as you can and sell them for what you can."

"But what about the birds that aren't worth anything?" she asked. "What'll you do with them?"

"I don't know," I said.

"Gator food," Louis interrupted, and Guy and I laughed along. I noticed that Tiger didn't laugh, but he didn't look like he was really paying attention anyway.

After breakfast, we hoisted a single sail and caught a damp, hot breeze up the river, toward Lettuce Lake. As we sailed, the river narrowed and closed in on us, so it soon felt as if we were going up into an alley of green. The farther inland we got, the more gators we saw. They were sitting along the banks and sunning, and every so often we'd see one disappear under the water as we approached. I knew gators were as scared of people as people were scared of them, but I sure didn't want to fall into this water.

Lillie and Tiger sat together on the bow, and Tiger pointed out different plants and animals we passed, giving her the Seminole name for each. He said the trees were called *E-to* and the alligator was *Hal-pa-tah*. The ducks we passed were *Fo-tso*, and once we heard a wild turkey in the bush that he called *Pen-e-wah*.

I only half listened, mostly because I was worried about Guy and Louis. They both had snored all night, and they were really sneezing and sniffling now. I hoped they would get better soon.

We sailed upriver for about a mile and a half, going slow, until the river opened into a shallow swamp. We almost grounded the *Magellan* twice looking for a channel through the swamp. Once we found it, we had to pole the *Magellan* through instead of sailing her. It was hard work, and me and Tiger did most of the poling.

Finally, we emerged from the swamp into Lettuce Lake. The lake was named for a particular kind of water plant that grew on its surface. The plant had rounded, flat leaves that sat on top of the water and looked a little like floating lettuce.

The whole surface of the lake looked solid —it was hard to believe there was actually water underneath all those plants—so I was surprised when we dropped anchor and found it was plenty deep. But we couldn't sail the *Magellan* through the thick plants. We'd have to take

Tiger's dugout canoe, which was just big enough for two of us.

When I mentioned this, Guy and Louis volunteered to stay behind, which I thought was a good idea. The last thing we needed was to scare away all the birds with their sneezing.

"OK," I said, "me 'n Tiger'll go…"

"Wait a second!" Lillie butted in. "I'm coming too!"

"What?!" I said. "No way! The boat holds only two people."

"It hold three," Tiger said, and I glared at my friend. I couldn't believe Tiger was taking my little sister's side! But Tiger was smiling a little bit, while Lillie looked like the cat that just ate the canary, as Mama would say.

"Fine," I huffed. "Let's just go."

We untied Tiger's canoe and lowered it into the water, then gingerly climbed down and loaded a few packs and shotguns into the canoe with us. Lillie tucked herself down in the middle of the little canoe and piled herself high with packs and ammunition boxes. It was close, but she fit.

Pretty soon, we pushed off from the *Magellan* and were heading across Lettuce Lake. The canoe was riding so low in the water that I was afraid a strong breeze would swamp us, but there were no breezes on the lake that day. No waves either. I'd never seen anything like Lettuce Lake—you could see the black water only if you pushed the swamp lettuce away with your hand or a paddle, and then the plants would come right back.

We got stuck more than a few times, and Tiger had to reach over the bow and free the clumps of swamp lettuce by hand. Every time his hand disappeared into the dark water, my heart rose in my throat a little bit. I already knew there must be gators in the lake, and maybe it was the heat or the bugs, but pretty soon my imagination started to run wild about what other kinds of monsters might live in those black waters.

"Hai!" Tiger hissed one time as he was clearing the canoe bow. He jerked his hand back so fast that the canoe rocked dangerously and a little water slopped in.

"Hey!" I exclaimed. "Watch out! You're gonna swamp us!"

Tiger looked frightened as a dark snake slithered away from the canoe, over clumps of the water lettuce Tiger had just been holding.

"*Chitto*," he said, still a little pale.

I had no idea what he meant until Lillie said, "water moccasin."

"Oh." I watched the big snake swimming away and shivered. Water moccasins were very dangerous snakes. Papa had told me they were

73

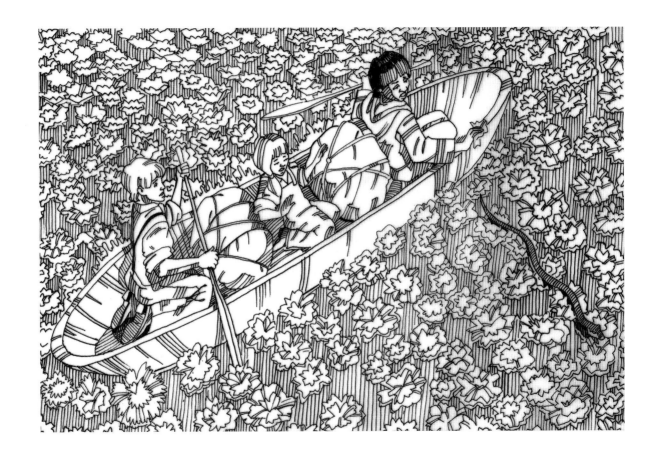

so aggressive they sometimes swam far out of their way to bite a person, and their bite was a strong poison that could make an adult very sick. If anybody got bit by a water moccasin now… I pushed the thought away and started poking at the water lettuce with my paddle just to make sure there weren't any more snakes.

It was almost lunch when we finally made it to the north shore of the lake and found a little dry land. We were all sweating and surrounded by great clouds of black flies. It felt great to get out of the canoe and walk in the shade of big trees, looking for a place to pitch a temporary camp. Lillie said we should find high ground because there'd be fewer gators and snakes away from the water. I agreed with her, but I didn't give her the satisfaction of saying so out loud.

We finally found a campsite and carried our supplies up from the boat. We decided to call it Camp Lettuce. We thought we still had time to hunt that afternoon, then cure the birds at Camp Lettuce and stay overnight. We'd be back at the *Magellan* first thing next morning.

The only problem was, I had no idea where to find birds.

"Look!" Lillie said, pointing up.

I followed her pointing finger and saw a large flock of birds coming up the lake, over the woods. I almost grabbed my gun to start shooting, but there were too many trees overhead, and I'd just be wasting ammunition.

"C'mon," I said. "Let's follow the birds and see where they're heading. Maybe there's a rookery around here somewhere."

Tiger and I grabbed our guns and headed off through the thick brush and forest, parallel to the lakeshore.

Chapter Nine

The Rookery

This forest was thicker and more wild than Hypoluxo Island, and the walking was made worse because Tiger and I were both weighted down with guns and as much ammunition as we could carry. Lillie was carrying some food wrapped in a bit of blanket in case we got hungry or had to pitch camp for the night.

The ground was marshy and muddy, and the mud sucked at our feet until our shoes were all covered with black gunk. I was a little annoyed because I was the loudest person in our expedition. Lillie and Tiger somehow managed to slip through the wet, wild marshland with barely a sound, while I clanked and spluttered along. If I was a plume bird, I would have heard me coming from a mile off.

We soon came across a small, sluggish creek, and the land rose a little. The brush thinned out, and we were soon walking among cypress trees the likes of which I'd never seen. Some of these ancient giants had trunks that were seven feet thick and the biggest knees I'd ever seen.

Cypress are interesting trees. Since they usually grow in water or on wet ground, where most tree roots would drown, the cypress makes its roots grow straight up out of the ground like big knobs surrounding the main trunk. These are called cypress knees, and they help the tree breathe. Most cypress knees around Hypoluxo Island were just a few inches high, but some of the cypress knees along this creek were up to my head. None of us, not even Tiger, had any idea cypress could get so big.

We followed the little creek, but it kept getting smaller until it finally disappeared altogether, and we climbed into a forest of cypress giants. The trees were so big that when we tilted our heads back and looked up, we could scarcely see the open sky far above. I felt a hush fall as if we were in one of Europe's grandest cathedrals.

"This is amazing," Lillie whispered.

I nodded. "Sure is."

And it was. The giant trees were cloaked with Spanish moss, so they looked like knobby old bearded giants from the picture books and fairy tales Mama read to us. I'd never seen any place so wild and lonely, but also so beautiful. Without even thinking about it, I reached out and took Lillie's hand, and she smiled at me. Even Tiger seemed a little awed by this example of God's creation.

We walked until the trees began to thin, and we saw more water through the cypress. I didn't know what this new water was called, but I hoped there were birds ahead. Then we heard the cries of birds, and my heart quickened.

Slowly, with Tiger in the lead, we emerged from the cypress forest and saw a small hammock of trees standing not too far off, with a pool of low-lying water extending from its base. The trees were buzzing with activity.

"A rookery," Lillie said happily. "Look at all the birds, Charlie. It's pretty, ain't it?"

"Isn't it," I automatically corrected, but she was right. It was pretty. The trees were draped with every kind and color of bird that I could imagine. There were birds in white and pink and black and blue and red, with big wings and short wings, long, curved beaks and short, sharp beaks. They fluttered up from their roosts and jostled along the thick branches in such great numbers that I could hardly see the trees underneath.

"Stay here, Lillie," I whispered.

For once, she listened.

I motioned to Tiger, and we crept forward. I'd never snuck up on a rookery before, so I didn't know how easily the birds would spook, but the last thing I wanted to do was scare away all those hundreds of birds. I figured that one rookery alone must have been worth a thousand dollars. Maybe more.

Tiger slipped his gun from his shoulder. "You go that side. I go this side," he said. He pointed, indicating that we should come at the birds from two different directions. This was the best way to hunt, because otherwise we might scare them all off in one direction.

"When I give the signal," I said, "start blasting."

Tiger nodded, looking excited.

We crept in different directions and finally positioned ourselves so Tiger was at 7 o'clock and I was at 4 o'clock, facing the rookery. We didn't want to be exactly opposite each other just in case one of us misfired.

I hid behind a palmetto bush while Tiger positioned himself on the edge of the swampy ground. I wasn't worried anymore about spooking the birds. They were making so much noise and flittering around so much that there was no chance they heard us.

When we were in position, Tiger watched me intently, his eyes glittering. Like me, he was laying out shotgun shells in a row so he could reload quickly.

Finally it was time. I got into my firing crouch and held up my hand and counted down with my fingers. Three. Two. One.

BOOM!

Our first blasts shattered the calm afternoon, but it was impossible to tell at first whether we got any birds. I quickly ejected the smoking shell, loaded another, and fired again. Then again. And again.

The birds took longer to react than I expected, and we got off several shots straight into the thickest part of the rookery. I figured they were making too much noise to hear us at first.

When they finally did react, they took off all at once, and the hammock looked like a volcano erupting feathers and birds. They flew in every direction, including right over me and Tiger. I got down on one knee and fired into the flock as it passed overhead. The sky was so thick with birds that their shadow passed over me just like a giant hand had passed across the sun.

It seemed as if it went on forever, but then it was suddenly over, and the last of the birds were out of range, flying straight and fast away from us. I stood up and shaded my eyes to watch them fly away, my gun barrel still smoking and red hot. My ears were ringing from all the shooting.

Tiger looked a little stunned, and I saw why. The ground all around us and the floor of the hammock were littered with bird carcasses. Lillie ran out of the woods and joined us, and she seemed shocked, too. She just looked at all the birds on the ground in great heaps.

"C'mon," I said to her. "Since you're here, you can help us pick 'em up." I handed her a sack, and we started picking up birds. Tiger joined us.

It took us nearly two hours to pick them all up, and I learned more about birds that afternoon than I had in my entire life up to that day. Lillie kept saying things like, "Look at this, Charlie! A great blue heron!" or "This is a scarlet ibis! Isn't it beautiful?" According to Lillie, we killed egrets and all different kinds of herons, including blue, white, green and Louisiana, along with ibis and cormorants. But no snowy egrets.

When we finally had them bagged up, the sacks were too heavy to carry, so we cut down a sapling and made a carrying pole. We tied the sacks to the pole and set off for camp with the sacks swinging between us.

My shoulders started to hurt right away, and the walking was even worse with the heavy pole digging at me. But I never uttered a single complaint. All I could think about right then was how much money was in those sacks and how the Great Plume Bird Expedition was probably the best idea I'd ever had.

Chapter Ten

Lillie Makes a New Friend

Cleaning and curing the birds was hard work, so we started as soon as we got back to camp. It was already late afternoon, and we had to work fast. I knew it was important to cure the plumes as soon as possible so that we wouldn't lose any.

To prepare the plumes, we had to skin and clean each bird, then soak the skin and feathers in a lime solution. After we soaked them, we hung them on tree branches to dry overnight.

By morning, they would be dry enough to pack for transport home.

While we worked, it quickly became obvious that we had more bird meat than we could ever eat. The pile of bird carcasses was soon as high as my waist, and pretty soon, Tiger had stopped cleaning birds and just stood looking at the pile of dead birds.

"Tiger?" I said. "What's wrong?"

"Enough birds here to feed my family for year," he said. "We should dry meat. Save it."

"But …" Then I stopped. I knew what he was saying. Tiger was a Seminole, and Seminoles hated wasting any part of an animal. They respected nature and all of God's creatures, and they never cut something down or killed something without thanking the plant or animal for giving its life to support them.

"Too many to cure," Tiger said, now sounding a little mad. "My father would be very angry."

I nodded because I knew that was true, too. I could only guess what Tiger's father—or any Seminole—would say about the huge pile of birds we had killed.

"Maybe we could dry a few?" I ventured, hoping to make him feel better. "As many as we can?"

Tiger nodded glumly. "I guess."

Lillie offered to help, and the two of them set to boning the little carcasses and setting strips of meat out to dry in the sun. I think we all knew they were barely going to make a dent in the big pile of dead birds, but it made them feel better, so I didn't say anything.

They left me alone to skin and clean and lime the feathers and skins. My hands were quickly raw and red from the caustic lime solution, and I sorely wished that one of them would help or that one of the Bradley brothers had come along to help out. But I didn't say anything.

The rest of the afternoon passed quickly, and we were all tired when the last of the sunlight drained away through the trees. I volunteered to make the fire and cook dinner if Lillie and Tiger would collect wood to burn. When they were gone, I looked around the campsite and realized what a mess it was. There were bits of feather all over the ground, and empty lime sacks, plus bones and that heap of bird carcasses. I understood what Tiger meant — my Papa was no Seminole, but he too talked about taking only what we needed from nature and leaving the rest for someone else.

Oh well, I thought a little defensively. I'm not the one who decided ladies want feathers in their hats. If it wasn't us, it would just be someone else.

I heard Tiger and Lillie coming back with a load of firewood. Tiger was piled high, but Lillie wasn't carrying anything. They were both smiling and laughing at something in her hands. As they got closer, I saw that she was carrying a tiny raccoon. It was no bigger than Papa's hand as it scampered along her arm.

"What's that?" I asked.

"We found him," Lillie said. "He's gonna help us eat all this bird. He likes bird."

Tiger fed the raccoon a little nibble of fresh bird meat. "*Wood-ko* like you too," Tiger said to Lillie.

"I'm gonna call him Bandit," Lillie said, grinning. "'Cause he looks like a bandit with the black band across his eyes. Can he can come with us?"

"Sure, sure," I said. "I just hope he doesn't bite."

"Be nice to him and he won't," Lillie said. "Right, Bandit? You won't bite Charlie, will you?"

The little raccoon looked at me and twitched his nose like he was considering biting me. We all laughed. I was glad the mood at camp was lifting, and I set about making the fire and preparing a feast of roasted bird meat, beans, and biscuits with a little huckleberry jam.

Chapter Eleven

The *Falcon*

We slept on the ground at Camp Lettuce. I was amazed to see that Bandit stayed with Lillie—I thought for sure he would take off into the woods, but instead he curled up next to her and lay with his black eyes glittering at the dying fire.

I was bone tired myself, so I fell asleep just as soon as I lay down, only to have Tiger shake me awake sometime later, in the darkest part of the night. I started to say something, but he clamped his hand over my mouth, and I came fully awake. He was crouched next to my blanket with one finger held up to his lips for silence. I started to get nervous.

He pointed to the big pile of bird carcasses.

"*Cat-sa,*" he barely whispered.

It took me a minute to see what he was pointing at, and then I almost screamed. Two big golden panthers had emerged from the dark and were helping themselves to the skinned birds. They were low to the ground and long, in the way that panthers are built, and their eyes glowed red in the dark. They ate with almost no sound at all except the crunching of bird bones that rattled across our camp like dry leaves in a wind.

I glanced at a shotgun and raised my eyebrows in question. These panthers weren't hurting us, but everybody knew that panthers could be very dangerous. It might be safer for us to shoot them.

Tiger shook his head no.

So we sat together in silence and watched the big cats prowling around the dead birds and eating. Once they had their fill, they vanished into the jungle without a sound, leaving behind only bones.

When they were gone, Tiger smiled at me and lay down. "Good luck, Charlie," he said. "We will have good luck from now."

I hoped he was right.

The next morning, the panther visit seemed like a dream, but the paw prints in the ground were very real. Lillie immediately got mad at us for not waking her up — "I wanted to see them too!" she yelled — but I told her to hush, and we broke camp.

I was unsettled that whole morning as we ferried our stuff back across Lettuce Lake to the *Magel-*

lan. Tiger and Lillie seemed happy enough as they fed scraps of meat to Bandit and Lillie peppered us with questions about the panthers, but I couldn't stop thinking about that big pile of bird carcasses.

Whatever worries I had were erased the moment we tied back up to the *Magellan* and started handing up bags and supplies to Guy and Louis, who had slept on the boat.

"Shoot!" Guy exclaimed, opening the bag of cured feathers and sniffling loudly. "Can you believe this, Charlie! This must be worth one hundred dollars right here!"

"A hundred dollars!" Louis exclaimed. "Man, I wish I could've seen that! I would've shot me a thousand birds! No, two thousand birds!"

"Well," I said cheerfully, "you might get that chance yet."

"So we're going back!?" Louis said. "We should go back…"

"No," I said. "There's no snowy egrets there. That's what we came for, and that's what we should get. We've only got so much ammunition. Remember, Samuelson said the snowy egret rookery is in Pa-Hay-Okee."

"Oh, alright! If you say so," Louis said.

Once we had everything stowed away, we lifted anchor to sail back down Cypress Creek, out the Hillsboro Inlet, and south. This time we were heading for Biscayne Bay, about thirty miles down the coast.

The day was crisp and clear, with a solid northwest wind behind us the entire voyage. Guy and Louis spent most of the day sitting on the deck, sniffling and coughing, while Lillie and Tiger put their hands in the spray and I steered the boat. We reached Biscayne Bay as night fell and cast our anchor for the night just inside in the protection of the bay.

The next morning, we ate a breakfast of dried bird meat and prepared to sail farther south. I had never sailed Biscayne Bay by myself, but according to my charts, it was thirty-five miles long. I figured we'd spend a day or two in the Bay and stock up on supplies before heading up the Miami River and into the great swamp.

As we sailed past the silent, wild shore, we passed only a few settlements, including old man Sturtevant's place. Some years after the Great Plume Bird Expedition, Mr. Sturtevant's daughter, Julia Sturtevant Tuttle, would buy land farther south down the bay and convince the great Henry Flagler to extend his railroad south from Palm Beach to Miami. This railroad would open up Miami to the rest of the country.

We spent the rest of the afternoon fighting headwinds and making little progress, and we ended up dropping anchor for the night just north of the mouth of the Miami River. It was another meal of dried bird, but I didn't complain because Tiger was still looking upset about all those wasted birds.

The wind was more favorable in the morning, so we continued on down to the mouth of the Miami River and reached the Brickell Trading Post. The Brickell post was the biggest trading post in Biscayne Bay—it served anybody heading north or south from the Florida Keys, as well as the Miami River. I figured John Samuelson, as well as every other bird hunter in the area, had probably stopped here.

After a few days on the boat, we were all grateful to get off and stretch our legs. William and Mary Brickell had built a large wooden house and a big dock along the riverfront, and it looked as if it could handle boats twice as big as the *Magellan*. There were already a few other, smaller skiffs tied up alongside the dock.

"Hullo, boys!" said a cheerful voice. We saw a woman coming out of the post and waving at us. When she saw Lillie, she added, "Hullo boys and girl! What can I do you for?"

I figured this must be Mary Brickell. She was known up and down the coast as a tough negotiator and good businesswoman. I tried to seem as grown up as possible as I introduced everybody while she stood shading her face from the sun. She seemed surprised to see a boatful of kids, especially including a little girl and a Seminole. She seemed even more surprised when I told her that we were planning to sail up the Miami River into the Everglades to find snowy egrets.

"You're planning to sail *that* up the river?" she asked, pointing to the *Magellan*.

"Yes, ma'am," I answered.

She shook her head. "You don't know much about the river here, do you, Charlie? There's rapids just up the river. You'll never get that boat up over those rapids. You could carry your little canoe, but that's about it."

I heard Guy and Louis mutter something behind me, and I felt my face burn a little. I was the one who had planned this trip, so I felt foolish for not knowing about the rapids. But Mrs. Brickell must have seen my disappointment because she considered for a second, and then she said, "But I might be able to help you anyway, Charlie."

"Really? How?" I said.

She pointed to a little skiff tied up against the dock. It was a light boat with a single mast that looked big enough for three people, plus supplies, but small enough that we could carry it if we had to. "I can sell you that little boat right there. She's called the *Falcon*. Matter of fact, it was another plume hunter that left it here in exchange."

"Oh," I said. "I don't know if we have that much money…"

"Well you must have something," she said. "You can't very well expect to get a boat for nothing."

I was still thinking when Lillie piped up behind me. "Charlie, what about all those plumes? Don't we have loads of plumes already?"

"Plumes?" Mrs. Brickell said. "That might work, depending on what you've got."

So we opened up the boxes and let her take a look at the plumes we'd collected at Lettuce Lake. They were dried and packed tight, but they hadn't lost any of their color. She looked pretty satisfied and told us that prices were still going up. Swallows and sea tern skins were fetching twenty-five cents apiece. Pelicans were worth fifty cents. A great white heron skin could get ten dollars, and flamingoes and snowy white egrets were worth an unbelievable twenty-five dollars.

"Of course, I don't see any snowy egrets, but you've got some good plumes here," she said. "I think we can make a fair deal all around, plumes for the *Falcon*."

We worked out an exchange, and I thought we paid a pretty fair price for the *Falcon*. Mrs. Brickell even said we drove a hard bargain.

This was the first time I'd seen how much plumes were worth. It was hard to believe we'd bought ourselves a little boat for just one afternoon's worth of work. If we could only find the snowy egrets, I was sure we'd have more than enough money to save our island.

After we finished our deal, we went inside the trading post to stock up on provisions and find some medicine for Guy and Louis, who were still keeping us awake all night with their snoring and sneezing. The post was a popular trading place, with a post office and shelves filled with all types of dried foods, hardware, and clothing. Mrs. Brickell also said that Seminoles often came down the river to trade with her. She had huge stacks of alligator skins and furs from the Seminoles, and she also stocked calico, beads, and utensils the Seminoles wanted. We bought canned beans, more ammunition, and splurged a little on rock candy. Lillie made everybody laugh when she let Bandit lick a little sugar from her finger.

I was also happy to find quinine and laudanum for Guy and Louis. Laudanum is a pain reliever made with opium, and quinine is a white, bitter, slightly water-soluble alkaloid obtained from cinchona bark. It was used to treat malaria, which was pretty common in the swamps. Guy and Louis took the medicine as soon as I handed it over, making faces at the bitterness and awful taste.

It wasn't long before we had loaded our new provisions back onto the *Magellan* and hooked up a towrope for the new *Falcon*. Mrs. Brickell wished us well as we cast off our lines and turned west, heading up the Miami River for the Everglades.

I was proud as we sailed up the river. I felt sure we'd meet with success now, and we looked like a real expedition with our new little boat bobbing behind the *Magellan* and the sails up to catch the afternoon breeze.

Chapter Twelve

Seminole Village

After we left the Brickell post and headed up the river, we passed a bunch of long, low buildings on our right. One of them, I knew, was the Dade County Courthouse, where Papa had come to record Lillie's birth certificate and the property deed for his extra land along the east side of Lake Worth. Back when these buildings were built during the Seminole Indian Wars, they were called Fort Dallas. It wasn't until later this area was renamed Miami.

We sailed on until we heard a rush of water ahead. Soon we could all see why Mrs. Brickell said we could never get the *Magellan* over the rapids. The river tumbled toward us down a bunch of small waterfalls, one after the other, stretching for about 50 feet. No boat could possibly sail up those rapids.

Tiger joined me at the tiller and said, "That's Pa-Hay-Okee." He pointed at the water. It was clean and clear. I started to get excited. We were almost there!

We found a small cove at the bottom of the rapids where we anchored the *Magellan*, and then we transferred our gear to the *Falcon*. It seemed like a pretty seaworthy little boat, and even loaded down with both Bradley brothers and Lillie, plus our gear, it didn't ride too low in the water. Tiger and I loaded more gear into his canoe, and we headed for the rapids.

It was slow, hard work to gain the base of the rapids, then unload our gear, carry it along the rocky bank, and go back and carry the boats. Even with all five of us dragging the *Falcon*, it still took the better part of the day, and we were all sweaty and tired by the time we got our vessels back into the water.

But we were excited, too, and even Louis, who had been complaining the whole time we carried the boats, hushed as we moved slowly up the river against the mild current. We were actually heading into the Everglades, and I wondered whether the others were thinking the same thing I was: How many rookeries are hidden in there? And where is Samuelson's secret snowy egret rookery?

But our search would have to wait because it would be night soon, and we would need a place to camp. Just as I was beginning to look for a good campsite, Tiger said, "Look," and pointed to thin columns of smoke rising into the sky from up ahead.

"What is it?" I asked.

"Seminole village," Tiger said.

I had been in a Seminole village before with Tiger, but none of the others had. Guy whistled softly as we rounded a bend and approached the village. The Indians wandered down to the riverbank to see who was approaching. The village was small, with thatched chickee huts sprinkled among more permanent structures made from wood. Two fires smoldered in stone fire pits, and a few little kids ran around the village, playing.

The Seminoles looked unhappy to see us until Tiger waved with his paddle and yelled a greeting in the Seminole language. Then smiles split their faces, and they invited us ashore to eat and spend the night.

As I climbed from the boat, I noticed a tall, regal-looking Seminole watching us. He had light gray eyes and was one of the finest-looking Seminoles I had ever seen. Tiger whispered "Jumper Osceola" in my ear. Jumper Osceola was supposed to be a descendant of Chief Osceola, the most famous of all the Seminoles.

We pulled our boats onshore, and Tiger introduced everybody. The Seminoles welcomed him like family and were very kind to the rest of us.

That night, the Seminoles prepared a feast of deer stuffed with vegetables and roasted over an open fire. They also served some kind

of bread I'd never seen before. When I asked about it, a look was passed among the older men. One leaned forward and said, "It's *conti hateka*."

"What's that?" Lillie asked around a mouthful of meat.

I cringed, worried that the Seminoles wouldn't like to be questioned by a young white girl with bad table manners. But the Seminoles just laughed. Lillie and Bandit had been a big hit earlier. She had Bandit do tricks like climb up her arm, and the little kids laughed and shouted "Wood-ko! Wood-ko!"

"*Conti hateka* is Seminole bread," Jumper Osceola said. "Made from special plant."

They then explained that the conti hateka plant was the same plant white men called *coontie*. The Seminoles used it to make bread by pounding the roots into a powder, then placing the powder into water and letting the starch sink to the bottom. They then used the starch to make bread. They said coontie plants used to cover all of South Florida until white men arrived. The white men used coontie plants to produce arrowroot, a starch we used in cooking. Once the white men discovered arrowroot, they dug up and killed almost all the coontie plants, and since it took thirty years for a single plant to reach maturity, there were no more young coontie plants to replace them.

"Now only conti hateka left is the conti hateka deep in Pa-Hay-Okee," Jumper said. "Where white man can't find it."

"That's awful," Lillie said, and she looked as if she meant it. But I didn't know exactly what I felt about the coontie story. On one hand, I felt a little guilty that my people had used up all the coontie plants. But I also knew that my Mama and Ma Bradley used arrowroot to make biscuits and cakes and other things I liked. It was a little confusing, to be honest.

After dinner, Jumper asked us why we were sailing up the Miami River in the *Falcon*. Tiger answered in Seminole, and Jumper frowned. Then he said something to Tiger, and Tiger listened but he looked at the ground. After Jumper was done speaking, I asked Tiger to tell me what Jumper had said.

Tiger looked pretty miserable as he said, "Jumper Osceola and Seminoles know the *Falcon*. White man sailed through here last month. He was plume hunter too. Jumper Osceola said boat was full of bird feathers, but bird meat and bones were left to rot in Pa-Hay-Okee. He said …" but Tiger stopped and looked embarrassed.

"What?" I asked. "What'd he say?"

"He said Seminoles stopped hunting for plume birds and no Seminole should hunt for plumes. He said my grandfather was proud warrior, that he is ashamed now that I am doing white man things."

I knew just what Tiger was talking about—and once again, I pictured that big pile of bird carcasses and remembered Papa saying that plume hunting was a lousy way to make money. But on the other hand, I also knew that we weren't the only plume hunters around, and the Seminoles didn't really understand money like we did. How could they be expected to understand that we needed money so we wouldn't have to sell our island? They didn't have any private land.

While all this was going through my head, Guy said, "But aren't there millions of birds? I've heard there are so many birds that sometimes they fill the whole sky. There's no way all those birds would disappear!"

Tiger shook his head. "Jumper Osceola said there were many coontie, too, and now there are few. He said that once white man starts to take, he takes until everything is gone."

I looked over at Jumper Osceola and the other Seminoles. They were watching us with hard expressions. I wanted to explain to them about Papa's land, but I knew they wouldn't understand. Instead, Tiger just looked miserable, and we went back to eating and didn't say much.

We slept in a chickee hut that night. Seminole chickee huts have thatched roofs and no walls. Their floors are raised off the ground so that no alligators or snakes can get in. Guy and Louis and I tried to make Tiger feel better, but he looked depressed and didn't say much. Even Lillie couldn't cheer him up with Bandit's tricks, including a new trick where she got Bandit to hide in her shirt collar and peek around her neck.

I didn't know exactly what to say, because I felt as if I understood Tiger a little better than my friends did. After all, Tiger and I had been friends since we were little boys. I knew that Tiger was a proud Seminole, but I also knew that he understood why we were plume hunting. That was the first time in my life I realized how hard it would be to live between two cultures, like Tiger was doing. He was Seminole, but I also knew he was proud of his friendship with me.

It was a long night that night, especially with Guy and Louis coughing and waking us up. That medicine I bought from the Brickell Trading Post didn't seem to be working.

I guess Guy and Louis must have been keeping the whole village awake because the next morning, a very old Seminole came to the chickee hut while we were getting ready to leave. He was wearing feathers and bones and carried a small bag that he pushed at Guy and Louis. They looked pretty nervous, but Tiger said, "It's Seminole medicine."

"I don't know," Guy said uncertainly. "Ma wouldn't want us taking anything like that."

Just then, he started coughing again, and Tiger said, "Looks like your medicine not working. Try."

So they boiled up a foul-smelling tea from the leaves and roots in the bag and drank it. Personally, I was glad I wasn't sick and didn't have to drink the stuff, but I hoped it worked.

After they finished with the Seminole medicine and we ate a quick breakfast, we prepared to leave. At the last minute, Jumper Osceola came down to the riverbank and said we couldn't take the *Falcon* that deep into Pa-Hay-Okee. Instead, he loaned us a big dugout canoe made from a hollowed-out cypress tree. I was surprised Jumper would help us after last night, but we were grateful for every bit of help we could get.

Chapter Thirteen

The Plume Hunters' Camp

The land flattened out as we headed up the river, and we soon entered the famous sawgrass marshes of Pa-Hay-Okee. Sawgrass is a very tall kind of grass with sharp edges like a serrated knife blade. It grows in the shallow water in masses so thick that you can't see even a couple feet in any direction when you're surrounded by it. I found out the hard way that it's also a bad idea to try grabbing sawgrass — the sharp blades stick into your hand.

We would have gotten lost in the sawgrass if not for Tiger. He showed us how to find the way through by looking for burn marks on the sawgrass. He said the Seminoles marked the sawgrass with flame, creating paths through the sawgrass swamp. It was easy for him to see the tiny marks, but none of us — not even Lillie — could find them so easily.

I knew the others were watching me to see whether I could lead them to Samuelson's snowy egret rookery, but the truth was, I had no idea where to look. I guess I had thought it would be easier to find a rookery in the sawgrass, but once we got there, it was such a huge space that I might as well have been searching the ocean for a particular wave. There were small islands of trees dotting the horizon, but they were all so far apart that we could spend a month going from island to island and see only a handful of them.

Still, I picked the very biggest island of trees I could see and said, "That one. We'll head there."

We pointed our canoes to that distant spot and started paddling.

The Everglades were unlike any place I had ever seen. The water was very clear and warm, but it was very shallow, and it moved slowly over the mucky bottom. I was used to the waterways at home and the inland swamps, but this was something else entirely. This was like a river of grass.

The whole time we paddled, Bandit scampered around the canoe and rode up on the bow. Lillie kept herself busy by feeding him and pointing out the fish that took shelter under our canoes. She wasn't much use with the paddle, but I guess that's just what little sisters are like, so I didn't say anything.

Sometimes, we heard larger things in the grass around us, and we saw more than a few alligators in the water. But mostly it seemed there were only water and grass and sometimes birds flying way overhead, much too high to shoot.

It took almost all afternoon, but we finally reached the big tree island. As we approached, I kept my eyes peeled, hoping to see the trees buzzing with birds just like the rookery at Lettuce Lake. But the trees were silent and still. Worse yet, there was a foul odor drifting from the island. It reminded me of the smell of a bear that had died on our island the summer before. We finally had to bury the carcass so we could breathe again.

I was filled with a strange dread as we pulled our canoes onto the shore and got out to explore. The smell was even stronger, and there wasn't a bird anywhere in sight.

"Oh my," Lillie said in a hushed voice. "Look."

"Ug," Guy said. "That smells even to me and my nose is plugged."

There was a stack of bird carcasses almost as high as my chest just inside the trees. They had all been skinned and thrown away, just like we had done at Lettuce Lake. I couldn't tell for sure what kind of birds they were, but there were a lot of them. Many more than we had shot.

"C'mon," I said. "Let's just look around, then we'll go."

We covered our faces with rags and explored the deserted plume hunters' camp, for that's what we had found. These plume hunters weren't nearly as careful as we had been at Lettuce Lake. They left empty pans and crates, broken utensils, and piles of shotgun shells all over the ground. Their fire pit was full of half-burned branches they had cut from nearby trees and tried to burn green, and plants and flowers were dead where they had carelessly thrown away their lime curing solution.

"This bad," Tiger said. "Jumper Osceola would not like."

"No," I said. "I guess you're right. We should get out of here."

We got back into the canoes and left the dismal, dirty camp behind. Nobody was talking much, and I wondered what they were all thinking.

It was the same thing every day after that. We would paddle to islands, going deeper and deeper into Pa-Hay-Okee, but every time, we found piles of dead birds and campsites where hunters had stayed. We slept on the damp ground at night and avoided islands that still smelled like dead birds. The only good thing that happened that week was that Guy's and Louis's colds went away. Whatever that Seminole medicine was, it had worked.

But everybody was getting angry and depressed about the lack of birds. Finally, after a week of finding nothing and eating beans, I got angry as well.

"I don't understand it," I said. "John Samuelson said he found a snowy egret rookery here. But how could that be? Every place here has been hunted nearly clean."

"He told you it was here?" Guy said, sounding doubtful. "Maybe he was lying."

I cast my mind back and tried to remember everything John Samuelson said. And then suddenly, like a light bulb going off in my head, I remembered him saying, "I'm coming up from way down past Miami." when he first saw us.

South of Miami!

Suddenly I figured it out. Samuelson wasn't here at all! He had come from farther south! I hurriedly explained what I was thinking, and my friends looked a little doubtful, until I went and got the charts and showed them what I meant. "See?" I said, spreading the chart out on the ground. "He came from farther south. Down here."

I put my finger on a place on the map all the way on the southern tip of Florida. It was called Cape Sable.

"I don't know," Guy said doubtfully. "That's pretty far away. It looks pretty wild down there."

"Sure it is!" I was excited now. "That's why there's still birds there! 'Cause it's wild! If we want to find these snowy egrets, I'll bet a pound of gold that's where we have to go!"

"You don't have a pound of gold," Lillie said.

"Not yet, but I bet if we go to Cape Sable, we just might!"

I could see that Guy and Louis were starting to nod along. It made sense, and I was convinced I was right: John Samuelson hadn't told the whole truth about his secret rookery. "OK," Guy said. "Let's try it."

I cheered, and we turned and headed back to the Seminole village. Guy and Louis seemed infected by my excitement, but I could tell from Tiger's expression that he was still unhappy. Lillie, too, had quieted down.

I knew what was bothering them. I didn't like the sight of those camps any more than they did. But whoever did that wasn't like us. We cleaned up our campsites, and we didn't take so many birds. And from now on, I promised myself, we would figure out a way to use all that bird meat, even if we had to salt it all and trade it.

We ate dinner that night with the Seminoles and returned Jumper Osceola's canoe. We didn't tell them about the camps, and they seemed happy we hadn't killed any birds. They sent us away with smiles the next morning as we loaded up the *Falcon* and headed back down the Miami River for a place that Guy had nicknamed "the end of the earth."

Chapter Fourteen

To the End of the Earth

It took us the rest of the day to get down the river and back to the rapids. I was glad to see the *Magellan* was still tied up safely where we left her, just below the rapids. But none of us were looking forward to carrying the *Falcon* back down the rapids again, and it ended up taking us until near dark. By the time we climbed back onboard the *Magellan*, we were all beat.

We decided to spend the night at anchor there and do some fishing for dinner. Louis was excited and got his fishing pole out. He quickly caught two large snook and three medium-sized redfish. Tiger managed to catch a small leatherback turtle that he used to make a delicious turtle soup. Afterward, we all sat on the deck and watched the moon rise over the trees and the stars come out. I don't know what the others were thinking, but I was thinking about all those empty rookeries and hoping that I hadn't made a mistake. I hoped I was right about Cape Sable.

We went to bed just after nightfall. After a week of sleeping on damp islands in Pa-Hay-Okee, I was happy to stay dry all night long. Unfortunately, a cold wind blew in, and I woke up in the middle of the night with my teeth chattering and my breath puffing out in white bursts of fog. It took a long time to get back to sleep.

The next morning, I woke up to splashing, and for one second I thought maybe Tiger had rolled off the deck and fallen into the river. But then I saw that he and Lillie were already awake, watching something huge in the water. I joined them and whistled in surprise.

Lillie looked at me with a huge grin on her face. "Look!" she said. "Aren't they pretty!"

Even Bandit was looking into the water with great interest.

A huge manatee was rolling in the warm water of the cove. It was almost ten feet long and wider across than the *Falcon*. Another one surfaced next to it, sending up a big spray with its giant flipperlike tail.

"They must be coming in for the warm water flowing down from Pa-Hay-Okee." I said.

Tiger nodded and pulled his shirt closer around him.

Louis and Guy woke up next and came up to watch with us. It turned out the whole cove was full of manatees, ranging in size

from huge, gentle giants to the little calves that stuck close to their mothers. They came right up next to the boat, but we didn't have anything to worry about—manatees are big, but they're harmless.

Once we warmed up in the morning sun, we decided to pull anchor and continue on our expedition. So we sailed through the manatees slowly, with Lillie counting them off the bow. In all, she counted 17 manatees in that one cove alone.

We stopped again at the Brickells' place to fill up with supplies and fresh water and so that I could get a chart and talk to Mr. Brickell about getting to Cape Sable. He was surprised to hear that we wanted to sail down the Florida Keys and over to Cape Sable at the bottom of the Florida peninsula.

"There's not much down there," he said, tapping the charts thoughtfully. "Just wide open water and mangrove."

I didn't say so, but that's just what I was hoping for. I knew from Papa and Uncle Will that Cape Sable was just about as wild and far-off a place as you could find in the United States and that, if you headed north up the Cape, you could find rivers and channels that led up into the heart of Pa-Hay-Okee.

"You ever get any plume hunters heading that way?" I asked, trying not to sound too interested, like I was just making conversation.

But Mr. Brickell wasn't fooled. "Plume hunters in Cape Sable? No sir, never heard of plume hunters that far south. I think most of 'em would be too scared to try something like that. You get in trouble in Cape Sable and you're in real trouble. In fact, I can't say that I've ever heard of anyone going to Cape Sable."

This was the best news I'd heard yet, and we all exchanged excited looks.

We sailed away from the Brickells' place with full casks of freshwater and high hopes. We were heading to a place where surely no plume hunters had been, a place where I was convinced we would find a rookery of snowy egrets.

Chapter Fifteen

Man Overboard!

It was midmorning when we waved good-bye to the Brickells and got under way. Once it warmed up, it was a fine day for sailing, and we stuck close to the shoreline. The water in the Bay was clear and pretty, with little waves washing against the *Magellan*.

About fifteen miles south of the Brickell place, we passed a piece of land sticking out called Black Point. Guy and Louis wanted to stop and shoot some birds, but I told them we were trying to save our ammunition, so we pushed on past and sailed until we came upon a huge mud flat that wasn't marked on the chart.

I had no idea how we were going to sail across the mud bank, so I told Lillie to climb up to the top of the mast and see if she could find a channel through. We zigzagged back and forth in front of that flat for another hour, with Lillie yelling, "There! No, wait. Forget it. There's a channel! Oh no. Sorry. Try this one!"

Finally, we got frustrated and just poled the *Magellan* across the mud, which was heavy and hard work.

After the mud bank, we finally got into deep water again and entered Card Sound. I'd seen a lot of beautiful water before, but Card Sound was just about the prettiest water yet. The Sound was twelve miles long and five miles wide and no more than ten feet deep, even in the deepest hole. The water was clear, like blue-green-tinted air, and you could see the bright fish darting between sea fans and sponges on the bottom. The shore of the Sound was thick with mangrove, and Louis proposed that we stop for some fishing.

"Those mangrove must be thick with fish, Charlie," Louis said, looking longingly at the shore. "Think about it. Barracuda. Snapper. Bonefish. You name it."

"Maybe," I said. "But we better keep going. We're going to need to find a good place to anchor for the night."

"Aw, come on," Louis said. "What could it hurt…"

"No, I want to get as far south as we can."

Louis didn't say anything else, but I could tell from the dirty looks he kept giving me that he was mad. He went to the stern so he could watch fish following us and probably dream about catching them. I wanted to go talk to him, but Guy said I should just let him be.

After a half hour or so, when I still hadn't heard anything from Louis, I decided to go talk to him. But when I climbed back, I didn't see Louis sitting on the stern where I expected him.

"Louis?" I called. "Louis!"

There was no answer. I thought maybe he was playing a trick on me and had snuck back up to the cabin to hide — maybe because he was still mad at me. But when we searched the cabin, there was still no Louis. That's when we really started to worry. We inspected every square inch of that boat looking for him.

Louis wasn't on the boat.

"He must have gone overboard!" Guy said, alarmed. "We've got to find him!"

"Louis! Louis!" we started shouting and scanning the water to see if we could hear or see him. But there was nothing except the sun glinting off the water.

"Hurry!" Guy said. "Turn around! We've got to go back!"

I rushed to turn the *Magellan* around so we could tack back up the way we had come. Lillie climbed back up the mast to look for Louis, and Tiger and Guy positioned themselves on either side of the bow and kept their eyes on the water. No one said it, but I knew we were all thinking the same thing. What if Louis was in serious trouble? A hundred awful thoughts crowded my head. He could have hit his head falling overboard. He could have gotten stuck in a current and been swept away.

"Shark!" Lillie suddenly sang out, and my heart started racing. "Look! A shark!"

I let the tiller swing free while we crowded at the rail and watched a big shadow glide under the boat.

"Bull shark," I gasped. Guy looked at me with such a worried expression that I felt as if I'd been hollowed out.

We stood looking at each other, and I could see in Guy's eyes that he was already thinking the worst. We all knew about bull sharks—they were the most dangerous sharks in Florida waters. To be honest, I was thinking the worst too, and it was probably the most scared I'd ever been in my life. I wished desperately right then that Papa or even Uncle Will was on board to tell us what to do.

"Charlie!" Lillie yelled. "Charlie! Look! There's something over there! In the water! HURRY! Quick, Charlie!"

From the deck I couldn't see where she was pointing, but I didn't waste any time turning the boat toward the place she was looking.

Guy and Tiger rushed up to the bow, and I sent a silent prayer up to God that everything would be OK.

Then we saw the most amazing sight I think I'd ever seen. A spotted dolphin swam right up to the *Magellan* and rose partway out of the water. It clicked and squealed at us a few times, then jumped high, turned around, and swam away a few feet. Then it popped out of the water again and waited for us to turn the boat. It wanted us to follow!

"Follow dolphin!" Tiger shouted excitedly. I didn't need to be told twice. It was leading us along!

Between Lillie yelling to hurry up and the dolphin leaping in front of the bow, I thought my heart might just beat out of my chest. But I was still unprepared for what I saw next: there was Louis, treading water! And there were more dolphins swimming in protective circles around him!

Tiger let out with a Seminole cheer, while Guy whooped and hollered on the deck and Lillie kept yelling, "We're coming, Louis! We're coming!"

In another minute, we hauled a dripping wet Louis on board like a big fish, and he stood there on deck looking tired and little sheepish. Turns out he had seen a big barracuda swimming along under the boat and leaned too far overboard to get a good look at it, then slipped right into the water. He paddled around for a few minutes, and then the dolphins showed up and swam next to him until we came around.

"They probably saved my life," Louis said.

"Did you see the shark?" Guy asked.

"Shark?" Louis said, his face going pale. "What shark?"

It seems, the dolphins had scared away the big shark and kept Louis safe the whole time we were looking for him!

I think we were all a little shaky with relief when I finally pointed the bow south again and we continued on our journey. It was already late, so we anchored along the mangrove shore, and Louis finally got his chance to do some fishing. In pretty quick order, he caught us two large mangrove snapper and a small grouper, and we had a fine meal of fish and pickled vegetables before we settled in for another night on the boat.

Chapter Sixteen

Into the Jungle

After another day of sailing and another night at sea, we made it to the top of the Florida Keys. The Keys are a long string of islands that kind of fall off the southern tip of Florida like bread crumbs. We'd all heard about the Keys, and it was tempting to keep heading south all the way to Key West, but instead we turned and pointed the *Magellan* west.

The water here was shallow and vivid blue, and it was soon clear we were entering wild country. On the map, these shallows were marked with names like Whipray Basin and Snake Bight, and it was difficult, slow sailing. The bottom of Florida isn't like a regular coast. It's really a maze of islands, creeks, and rivers where the Everglades flows into Florida Bay. In the three days it took to cross the peninsula, we didn't see a single other person or vessel of any kind. We hugged the coastline, feeling just about as alone as a group of people can feel.

While we didn't see people, we did see a profusion of wild animals. The water was teeming with big fish and schools of rays and sharks, and birds filled the sky in great flocks. Even our boat attracted visitors—huge clouds of black flies and mosquitoes descended on the boat and bothered us day and night.

"There must be a million rookeries in there," Guy said one afternoon as we watched the jumbled shoreline glide by.

"If only we can find a way in," I said.

On the third day, we sailed through Ponce de Leon Bay, which was named after the famous Spaniard who discovered Florida in 1513. There we found a promising inlet where a narrow river called the Shark River emptied into the bay. We pointed the *Magellan* into the river mouth and started to sail inland. It quickly became obvious this would be harder than we thought. Whoever drew the charts I was using to navigate had clearly never been on the river. The chart was all wrong, turning this way and that when the river turned every other which way, and there were whole islands that weren't even shown on the maps.

At one point, I got so frustrated with the chart that I said to Lillie, "I don't think whoever drew this map has ever even been here before!"

"Me neither," she agreed. "You think anybody has been here before? What if we're the first people to see this place?"

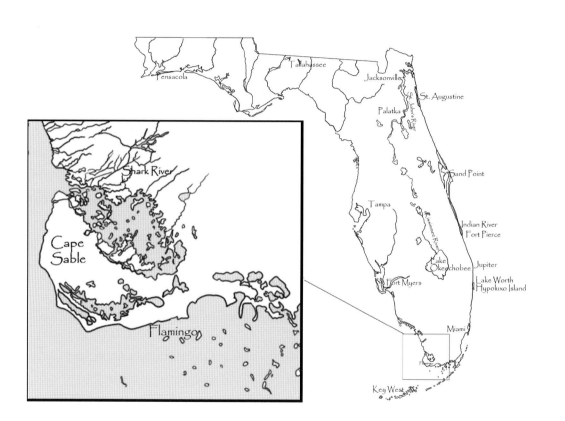

Pensacola

Tallahassee

Jacksonville

St. Augustine

Palatka

St. John's River

Sand Point

Tampa

Indian River
Fort Pierce

Kissimmee River

Lake
Okeechobee

Jupiter

Lake Worth
Hypoluxo Island

Fort Myers

Miami

Key West

Shark River

Cape
Sable

Flamingo

I hadn't thought of it exactly like that. I figured at least the Seminoles had been here, but Tiger said he'd never heard of a Seminole who traveled into Pa-Hay-Okee from the south.

"Seminoles don't go here," he said. "Too dangerous even for Indians."

I knew what he meant. We were at least three or four days away from the nearest help. Just like Mr. Brickell said, if we got into any trouble, we'd be on our own.

But for some reason, none of us was worried. I even had the feeling that someday I might tell my grandkids about the Great Plume Bird Expedition and the time we sailed into a place no person had ever seen before.

I was also mindful of why we had come here: snowy egrets. I figured John Samuelson might have made this very same trip to find his snowy egret rookery.

From that very first day on Shark River, we saw more birds than I had dreamed possible. They sometimes flew in flocks so great they cast a shadow over the sun, and we could hear them long before we could see them. These birds weren't afraid of human beings at all, which only convinced us further that we were the first hunters to have come this far.

We spent those first two days poling the *Magellan* up and down the little rivers. We took breaks sometimes to shoot birds, and we brought down all kinds of species, including cormorants, pelicans, blue herons, white herons, osprey, hawks, and eagles.

But we didn't shoot too many because Tiger refused to hunt with us and I was hoping to save our ammunition for snowy egrets, if we ever found any.

On the third day, I still felt as if we had only just poked our noses into the beginning of this place, and we still hadn't seen any signs of snowy egrets, so we decided to abandon the *Magellan* and take the *Falcon* and Tiger's canoe farther up into the shallow waters where the *Magellan* couldn't go.

We were traveling light now, with just the barest of provisions and as much ammunition and lime as we could manage. We figured we could get water from the river, and finding food was as easy as bringing down another bird or fishing for a few minutes.

We kept going farther and farther into the great swamp, passing islands and hammocks and rookery after rookery filled with common birds. But I wouldn't be satisfied now with anything other than snowy egrets, not after we'd come so far. I even started dreaming about snowy egrets, and I think the others were getting a little frustrated that I kept pushing us deeper and deeper into the swamp to find a snowy egret rookery.

Even Lillie couldn't figure out why I cared so much, and one day she asked me point-blank:

"Charlie, why are you so bent on finding these egrets? Aren't you surrounded by plume birds right now?"

"Yes, but I'm afraid they won't be worth enough," I said.

"Well who cares how much it's all worth?" she said. "Since when do you care so much about money anyhow?"

Maybe I shouldn't have, but that's when I told Lillie about Papa selling the island because we didn't have any Spanish gold left, about how Mama and Papa had spent the rest of the Spanish gold on her school and how after she ran away, they couldn't get any of it back.

Lillie's face fell after I told her this, and I felt a little guilty. But I figured she ought to know the truth.

That very next morning, we saw our first promising sign. A small flock of white birds flew overhead, going northwest through the tall grass toward a line of trees that rose up from the sawgrass. We were pretty certain these were snowy egrets, even though none of us had seen any in real life. But they looked like ones we had seen in the books. We excitedly took note of their direction and started to follow them.

The traveling got harder and harder as the sawgrass gave way to cypress trees and mud flats. We soon realized that even the *Falcon* couldn't navigate these choked waterways, so we decided

to abandon the *Falcon* and head on with just Tiger's canoe. We loaded all the remaining supplies into Tiger's canoe until there wasn't room for any people, and then we set off wading through warm, chest-deep water among the cypress with the dugout canoe in tow.

I had a feeling we were heading somewhere special, but it was hard to see through the thick trees to what lay ahead.

Chapter Seventeen

The Lost Village

This was the hardest traveling any of us—even Tiger—had ever done. The muck sucked at our feet, and our clothes weighed on us like stones. Flies and mosquitoes constantly attacked us, and there were plenty of animals around. Turtles watched us go by from their perches, we saw plenty of dangerous snakes, and more than once we saw alligators floating in the water nearby, with their eyes poking up to watch us.

"We don't want to be in this water come evening," Guy said, and everyone nodded in agreement. Alligators were pretty safe during the day, but anyone who lived in Florida knew they hunted at night.

It seemed as if we were in that water forever, until the ground began to rise and we gradually climbed up onto a solid spit of land. I had no idea whether this place could even

be called an island, but I guess that's what it was. It was thick with all kinds of trees — oak and gumbo limbo, wild cinnamon, and big palm trees — all ringed with huge cypress trees. Moon vines and creepers matted together overhead, and even the air seemed still and old and lonely, as if we were in some kind of green cave.

"Look," Lillie whispered. "Someone's been here."

We all crowded around to see the place she was pointing at, and our questions hung in the air. There was a trail on the ground, heading deeper into the forest.

"Maybe it's wild hogs," I said.

"No," said Tiger, who knew about such things. "Not *sok-a*."

"Well, we better check it out," Guy said.

We pulled the canoe far up onto dry land, loaded up three shotguns, and swung on down the trail, trying to be as careful and quiet as we could be. All the time we walked, my mind was filled with images of who could be this deep in the swamp. Tiger swore over and over that Seminoles didn't go this deep into Pa-Hay-Okee, and we'd never heard of any white people back up this far. So who could it be?

The trail went through dense jungle, rising slowly, until we came to a steep, short hill. It wasn't very big, maybe only a few feet, but it was an oddity nonetheless.

"You ever seen a hill like that?" Guy asked no one in particular.

"No sir," I answered. "Not a natural hill anyway."

We climbed up it only to find that we were on some kind of raised platform, a circle about thirty feet in diameter. The trees here were smaller and younger, as if this place had once been open to the sky above, and there was a huge pile of old shells in the middle, at least as high as my waist.

"Hey!" Louis called out. "Lookit this!"

He had picked up some kind of stone, except when we crowded around to look, we saw it was actually an arrowhead. It was made from some kind of flat stone that had been chipped into a sharp point.

"Only Indians made arrowheads like that," I said. "Tiger, are you sure this isn't Seminole?"

"Not Seminole," Tiger said stubbornly. "We no make arrowheads like that."

We scouted out the surrounding area and soon realized there were more huge shell piles scattered throughout the forest floor, along with stone rings for fires and poles that looked like they might have once held huts up above the ground. It was obvious that people had built this place and left behind these shell piles.

None of us could even guess how old this place was, but it felt very, very old. The shells were smooth and worn, and even though the trees were smaller, they were still grown up tall and strong.

"Boy," I said, trying not to get spooked about the idea of ghosts and spirits in this old village. "When we first came back here, I thought we might have been the only people to see this place. Now I kind of wish I still thought that."

"Look!" Lillie suddenly called out. "Charlie! Come here!"

We all rushed over to where she was standing in one of the smaller rings. She had found a fire pit—except this fire pit was different from the rest of the place because it had fresh ashes in it. There were still chunks of charred wood and new ash.

"Someone's been here," Tiger said, sifting through the ashes. "Soon."

Now it was impossible not to get spooked. But it was also late afternoon, and I knew for certain there was no way we could make it back to the *Falcon* that night. This was the only dry land we'd come across. We were stuck here, at least for the night.

"Let's build a fire," I suggested. "As soon as the dark starts to fall, we can take turns keeping watch. Just in case."

Nobody looked very excited about it, but I think everybody knew we didn't have a choice.

"OK," Guy said. "Let's get some wood."

We set out to collect wood, each heading in a different direction through the forest. There were plenty of fallen branches around, but we wanted only the oldest and driest branches.

This is just exactly what I was thinking when I walked down near the water's edge, far away from the others, and stopped in shock. The island ended here in a broad swath of sawgrass, and then another cypress forest. Even from this far away, I could tell these were the biggest cypress trees I'd ever seen. But more than that, one giant tree rose above the forest canopy, and this tree was glittering and buzzing with large white birds. I'd seen every kind of white bird I could think of so far—ibis and egret and heron—and by now I was almost as good as Lillie at picking them out and naming them.

These were snowy egrets, numbering in the thousands at least.

I was right after all. I'd just found the snowy egret rookery.

"Egrets!" I yelled, dropping my wood and dashing back through the woods to the campsite. "EGRETS! I FOUND IT! WE DID IT!"

They rushed after me, each staring in wonder at the rookery across the water. With the late afternoon sun shining on all those birds, they looked like dew sparkles.

"Wow," said Louis. "I bet there's ten thousand of 'em over there if there's one."

"Maybe more," Guy said. "There's enough there to make us all rich forever.

"Tomorrow," I said. "We'll get 'em tomorrow. But it's too late now, and I don't want to be wading through the water at night. First thing in the morning."

Tiger and Lillie didn't say anything as we went back to our campsite to build a fire for the night.

Chapter Eighteen

The Last Egret

We built a big fire near the biggest shell pile and sat around it. No one said much, but we all kept our guns close and kept our eyes peeled on the forest around us. As the dark fell, it seemed we heard all manner of noises in the water and the trees, and once we all jumped when Guy yelled "THERE!" and swore that he saw red eyes glaring at us in the dark.

"It's just an animal," Lillie said. "You act like you've never seen a raccoon in the dark." Bandit scampered across her arm as she said it and looked at Guy accusingly.

Guy just muttered and shifted closer to the fire.

"So are you guys really going to shoot those birds tomorrow?" Lillie asked.

"Yep," Guy said. "That's what we came all this ways for."

"But they're so pretty," said Lillie. "And we've barely seen any snowy egrets. I mean, I can understand you shooting the herons and things that we got close by home, but how do you know that's not every snowy egret left in the world?"

"That's just a girl thing to say," Louis answered. "Of course there's more'n just those."

"How do you know?" Lillie said. "Anyway, don't you think some things are just too pretty to be shot at?"

I could tell Lillie was getting herself worked up. I wasn't too worried about that, but I was worried about Tiger. He was staring gloomily into the fire. "C'mon, everybody," I interrupted. "It's getting late. We better turn in for the night."

Tiger volunteered to keep the first watch, so the rest of us arranged our blankets in a circle around the fire, head to toe and head to toe, and went to sleep. I woke up when it was my turn to keep watch and sat wrapped in my blanket. The fire had already died down to embers, and I jumped at every night sound. I was startled once by glowing red eyes from across the fire until I realized it was only Bandit staring at me from where he had nestled next to Lillie.

I was just dozing off when I was jerked awake again by a sad, singular cry. I couldn't tell where it came from or what had made it. It sounded like a bird, but it was deeper and

echoed through the forest. I thought it was just about the saddest sound I'd ever heard, and I had a hard time falling back to sleep after that. I wondered what kind of animal sat up at night in the middle of all this great, beautiful, lonely swamp and made such sad cries.

The next morning, I woke up to the sound of loud, angry voices. I sat up quickly and saw Tiger and Lillie squared off against Guy and Louis. Everybody was arguing with each other.

"Give it back!" Guy said, grabbing for Lillie. But she danced backward, out of the way. I jumped up and ran over to see what was going on.

"She's got the bag of shells!" Guy said as soon as I came up. "She says she's gonna throw 'em in the water if we leave to go kill them snowy egrets!"

"You shouldn't kill those birds!" Lillie said hotly. The pouch full of shotgun shells was hanging behind her back.

"Lillie!" I said. "Give back the shells! What are you doing?! You can't take our shells."

"We don't think you should go hunting today!" Lillie said. Her face was stubbornly set, and I recognized the expression from when she ran away from school.

"We?" I said. "Who's we?"

"Me 'n Tiger," Lillie said. "Right, Tiger?

Didn't you say they shouldn't kill any more birds?"

Tiger looked miserably at the dirt and didn't answer. But I could tell from his expression what he thought.

"You didn't really say that, did you, Tiger?" Guy demanded. "'Cause that would be just stupid. We came all this way to get plumes, so why would you just give up like that? Now give back those shells!"

"No!" Lillie said. "Tell 'em, Tiger! Tell 'em what you said!"

"No," I said. "It's alright, Tiger. You don't have to come."

Tiger looked up at me, and there was relief on his face. But something else, too. He looked upset.

"But you know we've got to go?" I said. "Right? You know that?"

Tiger didn't say anything, but he shook his head just a tiny bit from side to side, and it was just as good as if he'd yelled, "YOU DON'T HAVE TO GO!"

Angry now, I turned to Lillie. "Give me the shells, Lillie. Right now."

"You ain't Papa, Charlie," she said. "You can't boss me around any way you want. We say you shouldn't go. We say…"

"Lillie," I said quietly. "I told you why we need that money. Now give me back the shells. Or whatever happens'll be on you."

I knew it was a cheap shot as soon as Lillie's eyes filled up with tears. But I was too angry just then to care, and I snatched the big sack of shells away from her as soon as she offered it.

"Now c'mon," I growled at Guy and Louis. "Let's go."

Neither Tiger nor Lillie said anything as we loaded the canoe. We set off into the warm water, wading across the half mile of sawgrass to find the snowy egrets. I don't know what Guy and Louis were thinking, but it was with a heavy heart that I waded through the slowly moving water toward the big tree where the snowy egrets buzzed and fluttered.

It took us the better part of three hours to cross that section of sawgrass. There was a deeper channel in the middle, so we had to swim across one by one and then rig the canoe on a line and pull it after us. After that, we still had another hour of wading ahead of us, and sometimes the sawgrass grew up so tall that I knew which direction we were heading only by looking at the sun overhead.

Finally we started to climb into shallower water and saw the first trees of the cypress forest that sat between us and the rookery. We got our first good look at the rookery, and Louis was right: there were more birds there than a person could count. The whole tree was covered with them, as if it were wearing a white coat that shook in the heavy breeze. Even from this distance, the white of the plumage was dazzling beyond description.

Then we headed into the cypress forest. We had seen some beautiful woods before now, but nothing like this place. The cypress soon gave way to fig trees that had buttress roots as tall as my head and more roots hanging down to latch onto the ground like so many legs. And there were gumbo limbo here, too, with their trunks and branches bright red and peeling like sunburned skin. As we climbed higher, we entered a stand of live oak that was hung with Spanish moss like an old man's beard, and orchids and air plants clung to the trees' rough bark. It was like a fantasy described in a fairy tale, and I half expected the flowers and trees to come to life and start talking to us.

I'd lived in wild places most of my life, but I'd never seen a place like this. It almost seemed like God was showing off his beauty and magic, and I wondered if the snowy egrets chose this spot for their rookery because it was the most beautiful place on earth.

We cleared the last of the oak and headed back into the water, toward the tiny island where a single huge tree towered above the surrounding landscape and was covered with snowy egrets. Suddenly, in the presence of all that majesty, I was overcome with doubts. What if Lillie was right? What if these were the only snowy egrets left in the world? I remembered Jumper

Osceola's face as he talked about the coontie and the plume birds. He was angry, but it was more than that—he was sad, too. Some things, once they're lost, you can never get them back.

I tried to shake my head clear as Guy and Louis and I figured out the best way to attack the rookery. Just like before, we wanted to set up shooting angles, so that we could get as many birds as possible, as fast as we could.

"I bet we get five hundred birds!" Louis said excitedly.

But all I could picture was five hundred skinned carcasses piled up back at camp and Tiger looking at me over the fire with the same expression on his face that Jumper Osceola wore.

"You OK, Charlie?" Guy asked quietly.

I looked at him and tried to grin, but it came out a little wrong. "Sure," I said. "Let's just go."

We waded out and split up to take our positions. Just as we did at Lettuce Lake, the others were supposed to wait for my signal so that we could all start firing at once.

I crept quietly through the sawgrass until I reached shallow water near the rookery. Guy and Louis were wading into position also. I took my time loading up the first shell and arranging my pouch with fresh shells. Then I looked up at the tree and really saw snowy egrets up close for the first time. I'd never seen a bird as dazzling white, with such large and breathtaking feathers.

Many of them were sitting on nests, and I could hear tiny chicks peeping at their parents.

It was as if the orchids of the jungle had come to life, and then, for no reason in particular, I heard Papa's voice in my head, saying, "I don't want to be killing things we don't need to kill." I remembered how the Seminoles looked around their fire, talking about how white men had destroyed all the coontie plants, and I remembered how all those camps in Pa-Hay-Okee had smelled when they were full of dead birds.

I knew that if we shot these birds, we'd end up creating another pile of dead birds that we couldn't eat and leaving all those chicks to die—just so a bunch of ladies I never met could put feathers on their hats. I had been raised to eat what I killed, not to throw away God's creations like so many used rags.

I could feel the frustration rising. It seemed that every person I loved and respected—my Papa, Tiger, the Seminoles, even Lillie—was lined up in my head, telling me this was wrong. And the only person who thought it was right was John Samuelson, a man I hadn't even liked very much when I met him.

I felt as if I was making a choice: did I want to grow up to be a man like Papa or a man like John Samuelson?

That was the final straw. Before I could think about it any more, I raised my gun up, straight up into the air, and let a blast go into the blue sky.

There must have been something in that first shell I loaded, because it was the loudest shotgun blast I'd ever heard. The echo rolled across the open swamp and seemed to bounce around in the trees for a minute or more.

All at once, the white coat of birds covering the massive tree seemed to lift up in the air like it was shedding a skin. The egrets hung in the air for a single heartbeat, so white they almost glowed, and then the birds streaked off in every direction.

"HEY!" Louis yelled, and he managed to get off three or four blasts at the fleeing birds, but I didn't see any fall. I smiled at the sight of Louis running back and forth at top speed, trying to load while he was still running and aiming at birds but not hitting any. Guy, too, was smiling, sitting with his gun draped over his arm. When our eyes met, he nodded at me as if to say he understood what I had done.

The flock filled the sky for only a minute, with the early morning sun glinting off their glorious, valuable plumage, and then in an instant, they were gone, the last egret streaking away across the great Everglades.

Epilogue

In all, we were gone for five weeks on the Great Plume Bird Expedition. When we returned, Papa was steaming mad, and I thought at first he was going to put me over his knee and get out the switch. But before he did, he told me to explain everything, that I ought to have a chance to defend myself.

I could have come up with some story, but instead I told Papa the whole truth. I told him that I didn't agree with him at first about plume hunting, that I thought we could make enough money hunting birds to save the island. I told him about planning the trip, and how we loaded up on supplies and sailed down to Lettuce Lake, then to the Seminole Village, and finally to Cape Sable to find snowy egrets.

Then I sat thinking for a few minutes, looking for the right words. "But I couldn't shoot 'em, Papa," I said. "I was right there, and we had the birds in our gun sights, but then I heard your voice in my head, and I ... I guess I realized you were right." I hung my head. "I'm sorry. I truly am."

He nodded his head, and even though he was still mad, he smiled at me. "I'm glad to hear it, Charlie Pierce," he said. "You're at the age now when you're about to grow up into the man you're going to be, so it's time to start making grown-up decisions."

I felt good, but I was still troubled, and Papa asked me, "What's still on your mind?"

"Well," I said. "Here's the truth, Papa. We might have been the first people up Shark River that far, but we won't be the last. I saw those camps in Pa-Hay-Okee, by the Seminole village, and I just think that soon that place we saw with the flowers and the oak trees will look just that same way. Full of dead birds and spent shell casings. With no snowy egrets anywhere in sight."

"It might," Papa said sadly. "Sometimes you might know a train is coming, and you can even see it from a long ways off, but that doesn't mean you can always stop it."

"It doesn't seem right."

"No," Papa said. "It doesn't."

We did bring some plumes home from that trip — about $800 in all. We split it three ways, because Tiger didn't want any part of it, and I gave the money to Papa just like I promised I would.

Louis used his share of the money to buy himself a little skiff that he fished from. Pretty soon, he was known as one of the best fishermen anywhere around Lake Worth. He told everybody that was because he had swum with dolphins and they told him all their secrets.

We were far from the last plume hunters in southern Florida. There is no way to describe the plume trade in those years except to say that people were consumed with their greed. When we returned from our trip, snowy egrets were already selling for almost one hundred dollars a bird. And the demand only went up from there. In New York, they piled the ladies' hats higher and higher with plumes until you couldn't hardly see the ladies' heads underneath all those feathers.

And they used every kind of bird you could imagine. I learned much later that sixty-four species of birds were hunted for their plumage, and most of those came from the Florida Everglades. I was right, too, about what would happen to the birds. It turned out that shooting birds in rookeries was like a two-for-one in terms of killing. Those birds were mating, so many of them were sitting on nests. Once the birds were shot, there was no parent to protect the egg, so the eggs and the chicks died, too. The hunters were killing two generations of birds, not just one.

But there was no stopping the engine of commerce. Plume hunting was big business and only getting bigger. By 1903, the price for plumes had reached up to thirty-two dollars per ounce, which was twice the value of gold per ounce.

Later, it would hit eighty dollars an ounce. Around that time, 83,000 people worked in the hat trade, or one out of every thousand Americans. There was some outcry over the slaughter in the Everglades, but the hat makers up north just said they collected only feathers that had already fallen off birds.

Of course, we who had seen the camps knew better.

In 1886, a group was created called the Audubon Society, named after the bird artist whose paintings Mama had cherished. The Audubon Society published magazines, offered lectures, and organized groups of wealthy ladies to give up their hats and convince others to do the same. Pretty soon, Audubon Society chapters were established all over the country, and the society was a major voice in the protection of birds.

But it wasn't enough, at least not in those early days. One by one, birds started to go extinct in the Everglades, just as I had feared that morning.

Of all of us, I think this was hardest on Guy. I don't know what exactly changed in him after our expedition, but he started learning more and more about the Everglades and the birds and animals that lived there. Later on, he used his share of the plume money to buy a piece of land in Flamingo, near Cape Sable, and was hired as a game warden. He spent the rest of his life tracking down and arresting plume hunters in the very same region we hunted in as teenagers.

I sometimes wondered whether he ever visited that forest we saw and if it still looked the same.

I wish I could say that Guy won his battle against the bird hunters, but it wouldn't be true. The forces against him were too powerful, and I learned the hard way exactly what Papa meant when he said these men wouldn't let anything stand between them and their profit.

On July 8, 1905, my friend Guy was shot in the throat by a plume hunter who was illegally shooting birds. Guy was trying to arrest the hunter, but the man was willing to commit murder to keep his illegal profits. It was an awful tragedy, and I thought no good could come from such a thing. But Guy's

Guy Bradley, 1870-1905, was a game warden hired to protect birds in the Everglades. *Photo from The Historical Museum of Southern Florida*

murder caused people all over the country to sit up and pay attention to the plume hunting in the Florida Everglades. When they found out what was happening, ladies all over the country started letter-writing campaigns, and pretty soon it was no longer fashionable to be seen wearing plumes. Finally, in 1918, the United States passed the Federal Migratory Bird Treaty Act, which protected these beautiful birds forever.

None of this brought Guy back, but I think maybe Guy would be pleased that some changes were made because of him. And it turned out that Guy made the history books. He was America's first conservation officer killed in the line of duty, and decades later a historic marker at the Visitor Center at Everglades National Park near Flamingo was erected in his honor. Guy Bradley is a hero.

As for my family, we were able to hang onto Hypoluxo Island after all —even though Mama never did get any blueberries from her little patch. In the few years after our Great Plume Bird Expedition, land values started to rise fast in Florida as more people discovered our paradise, and Papa ended up making a small fortune off his "bad" investments on the barrier islands. Turns out Papa sold his land to that oil tycoon Henry Flagler, who created a winter resort, called Palm Beach, for the rich and famous.

As for me, I never killed another plume bird again.

About Charlie Pierce

Charles William Pierce was born in Waukegan, Illinois, in 1864 and moved with his parents to Jupiter, Florida, in 1872 at the age of eight when his father was given the job as assistant keeper of the Jupiter Lighthouse. At the time, the geographical area that today comprises Palm Beach County was still part of Dade County (Palm Beach County was not created until 1909) and was inhabited only by Native Americans and escaped former slaves. The only white residents were the keeper and assistant keepers of the Jupiter Lighthouse. The Pierce family homesteaded Hypoluxo Island in 1873. In 1876, Charlie's father served as the first keeper of the Orange Grove House of Refuge, located in modern-day Delray Beach, where the Pierce family housed sailors shipwrecked along the beach. It was here that Charlie's sister, Lillie, was born in August 1876. She was the first white child born between Jupiter and Miami, an area that contains approximately seven million people today. Pierce grew up in the jungle wilderness that was South Florida prior to the arrival of Henry Flagler's Florida East Coast Railroad some two decades later. The Pierces' were one of the three families that salvaged the 1878 wreck of the *Providencia*, a Spanish ship carrying twenty thousand coconuts. The Pierces helped plant the coconuts that would later give Palm Beach, West Palm Beach, and Palm Beach County their names. During his long, illustrious life as a pioneer settler of South Florida, Pierce served in many capacities, most notably as one of the legendary barefoot mailmen who carried the mail

Left to right: Margretta M. Pierce; Hannibal D. Pierce; Andrew W. Garnett; James "Ed" Hamilton; Lillie E. Pierce; and Charles W. Pierce at the Pierce family home on Hypoluxo Island, ca 1886. *Photo courtesy of Historical Society of Palm Beach County*

from Palm Beach to Miami and back each week. In all, the barefoot mailmen covered 136 miles

The mailman in this mural titled *The Barefoot Mailman*, by Steven Dohanos, is said to resemble Charlie Pierce. *Photo courtesy of Historical Society of Palm Beach County*

proximately seven thousand miles per year. They were paid six hundred dollars per year salary. Pierce served for more than forty years as the postmaster of Boynton Beach, moving to Boynton Beach in 1895, more than twenty years before the city was first incorporated. His son, Charles, was the first child born in Boynton Beach. Pierce served on the boards of various community organizations, as president of the first bank organized

round-trip in six days, rested on Sunday, and then started anew on Monday, for a total of ap- in Boynton Beach, and as master of the first Masonic lodge. His childhood adventures were accurately recorded, and his writings remain today one of the best first-hand accounts of early exploration in southeast Florida. Pierce was farsighted enough to maintain a daily journal from early childhood until late in his life. These journal entries provide the foundation for his book, *Pioneer Life in Southeast Florida*, which is the most comprehensive account of the pioneer settlement of south Florida and the primary reference for most subsequent books on the region's history. Pierce died in 1939, at age 75, while still serving as the postmaster of Boynton Beach. Pierce Hammock Elementary School in Palm Beach County is named in his honor. In 2009, the State of Florida posthumously named Charles

Charles Pierce at his desk, ca 1930. *Photo courtesy of Historical Society of Palm Beach County*

Pierce a "Great Floridian," one of fewer than fifty people in Florida's history granted the title. Florida Governor Charlie Crist performed the induction.

About the Author

Harvey E. Oyer III is a fifth-generation Floridian and is descended from one of the earliest pioneer families in South Florida. He is the great-great-grandson of Captain Hannibal Dillingham Pierce and his wife, Margretta Moore Pierce, who in 1872 became one of the first non-Native American families to settle in southeast Florida. Oyer is the great-grandnephew of Charlie Pierce, the subject of this book. Oyer is an attorney in West Palm Beach, Florida, a Cambridge University-educated archaeologist, and an avid historian. He served for many years as the chairman of the Historical Society of Palm Beach County and has written or contributed to numerous books and articles about Florida history. Many of the stories contained in this book have been passed down through five generations of his family.

Harvey E. Oyer III

For more information about the author, Harvey E. Oyer III, or Charlie Pierce and his adventures, go to **www.TheAdventuresofCharliePierce.com**. Become a friend of Charlie Pierce on **Facebook.**

Atlantic
Ocean

Jupiter Lighthouse
Brelsfords' Store
Pierce Homestead
Orange Grove House
of Refuge

Hillsboro River Inlet

Miami
Brickell Trading Post
Key Biscayne
Biscayne Bay
Card Sound

Bradley Homestead
Hypoluxo Island

Cypress Creek

Miami Inlet
Seminole Village
Miami Rapids

Shark River
Flamingo

Lake Okeechobee

Everglades
Pa-Hay-Okee

Kissimmee River

Cape Sable

Gulf of Mexico

Key West

MAGELLAN

The Adventures of Charlie Pierce: The Last Egret

is generously provided by Wells Fargo in association with:

The Historical Society of Palm Beach County

The School District of Palm Beach County

The Arthur R. Marshall Foundation

Together we'll go far

© 2010 Wells Fargo Bank, N.A. All rights reserved. Member FDIC. ECG-341003